DEAD R

MW00473619

A Review of Horror and the Weird in the Arts
Edited by Alex Houstoun and Michael J. Abolafia

No. 33 (Spring 2023)

DEAD RECKONINGS is published by Hippocampus Press, P.O. Box
641, New York, NY 10156 (www.hippocampuspress.com). Copyright
© 2023 by Hippocampus Press. Cover art by Jason C. Eckhardt. Cover
design by Barbara Briggs Silbert. Hippocampus Press logo by Anastasia
Damianakos. Orders and subscriptions should be sent to Hippocampus
Press. Contact Alex Houstoun at deadreckoningsjournal@gmail.com
for assignments or before submitting a publication for review.

ISSN 1935-6110   ISBN 9781614984092

Wicked and Wonderful Celtic Folklore

Daniel Pietersen

Celtic Weird: Tales of Wicked Folklore and Dark Mythology. Edited by Johnny Mains. London: British Library Publishing, 2022. 336 pp. £14.99 tpb. ISBN: 9780712354325.

One of the challenges with tackling a collection of Celtic traditions and folklore is that the word, and the world associated with that word, is far broader than may be first imagined. At their height, the various Celtic peoples covered vast swathes of western and central Europe, yet they were linked largely by speaking an intermingled family of languages rather than any ethnic or cultural ties. Even the modern Celtic nations, which sweep down the west coast of the British Isles and on into the Breton Peninsula, share a group of interrelated languages and distrust of their oft-invasive neighbors far more than any fraternal solidarity. The Celtic tradition of storytelling, shared characters, and plots rising and falling depending on the teller's whim is more akin to a churning cauldron of narrative than a formal, indexed (some may say less exciting) library. And all this before we've even tackled what we mean by "weird" . . .

In his introduction to this anthology, editor Johnny Mains manages both to acknowledge and to wave away this challenge by stating, not incorrectly, that "Celtic myths and folklore have always been extremely weird." This is evidenced by the eerie characters of Celtic tales and their capricious personalities as much as it is by the way those tales ooze and flow between different traditions; similar nations, with the raging sea on one hand and an oppressive neighbor on the other, tend to have similar concerns, after all. Such an approach allows Mains to wield a broad brush that wanders across almost two centuries of storytelling and accepts tales about the Celtic nations (Scotland, Ireland, the Isle of Man, Wales, Cornwall, and Brittany) as well as entries written by natives of those lands. While this may upset purists, I feel it gives a more holistic view of places where—and I speak as an adopted resident of Scotland and a one-time lurker on the Welsh-English threshold—the concept of outsiderdom is more rigidly enforced but also much more fluid than elsewhere.

Robert Aickman's "The Fetch" is a prime example of what Mains calls these "welcome interlopers." The story's soul itself is slight—the narrator's family is haunted by the carlin, or hag, of Scottish myth, whose appearance predicts (perhaps causes) the untimely death of loved ones—but it is Aickman's "deeply uncanny" writing, as Mains puts it, that lifts the narrative into something much more unsettling. Brodick Leith, Aickman's narrator, is pushed and pulled by the carlin's ebbs and flows: between bustling London and dreary Scotland; between the women he loves and the "wraith" of a father he avoids. Aickman works at our sympathies as Leith unexpectedly finds a happiness that, equally unexpectedly, falls through his increasingly listless fingers. Yet throughout the story the single common factor of the carlin's appearances is Leith himself. He glimpses her in the distance or, chillingly, hovering outside upper-floor windows. Aickman, always adding layer after layer, makes us wonder whether the carlin exists to bring death to Brodick's family or to shield him from a life he finds too difficult.

This brush with death, and the confusion as to whether it is willing or not, reappears in "Shepherd, Show Me . . ." by Rosalind Wade. Set largely in the grounds of a house known as Lancevearn—one of the type that crouches at the end of the long, winding roads that snake across Cornwall—Wade's tale tells us of an unwilling glimpse into the strange ways in which people fall into grief, a grief that is mentioned as little in the narrative as it would be in the characters' strait-laced lives. An oblivious husband, sinister interlopers, a weird link between the present and the past: these are fine but not unusual elements for a chilling tale; but what is unusual, and all the more unsettling because of it, is that Wade's unnamed narrator and unwilling investigator suddenly understands what is happening almost as we, the readers, reach the same conclusion. She stands on a lonely cliff-path "with the wisps of grey mist clinging to the vegetation and the leaden sky above" and terrifies herself with her own realization, the cliff's crumbling edge only adding to the vertigo that blurs character and reader.

The absolute gem of this anthology, however, has to be "The Green Grave and the Black Grave" by the American-born Irish writer Mary Lavin. To call this a story is to do Lavin's work a huge disservice; it sits somewhere in a nebulous realm between poem and dream with the sing-song cadences of two Irish fishermen, father and son who know each other's ways intimately, transformed into a ritual chant, a hymn to death and sorrow and loss and being lost oneself. Lavin's choice of words, flowing and fickle, tells us more about the sea—a sea to whom "life or death, it was all one thing in the end"—than any description ever could. We learn how deep the sea has soaked into the being, into the soul, of these island people by the crests and hollows of their words, by their philosophy as solid as ocean waves. We learn the litany of those men—other fathers, other sons—who are caught "by the green sea grasses and the green sea reeds and the winding stems of the green sea daffodils" as their wives lament their loss; "it would be hard to know by their keening whether it was for their own men or the men of their neighbours they were keening." "The Green Grave and the Black Grave" is beautiful and bleak and haunting and horrible and deeply, deeply sad in way only reading it could make you understand.

As with every collection, however, not every tale held here landed as well with me. "The Knight of the Blood-Red Plume" by Ann of Swansea employs a tiring faux-medievalism, replete with sighing maidens and pensive knights, which starts to grate long before its twist is eventually revealed. Edith Wharton's "Kerfol" depicts a bleak and depressing misogyny that, while realistic and deftly portrayed, saps at the quiet eeriness of its genuinely unique opening scenes. Yet these are only a few tales in a book that falls open far more often on tales I genuinely enjoyed: "Mermaid Beach" by Leslie Vardre (pseudonym of L. P. Davies) and its one-two jab of an ending; the oneiric journey of Eachann MacPhaidein's "The Butterfly's Wedding"; Eleanor Scott's out-weirding of M. R. James on the haunted Breton shores of

"Celui-Là." No doubt other readers, too, will prefer some rather than others, as is natural in such a wide-ranging anthology.

I can't end this review, however, without a mention of *Celtic Weird* as a quite beautiful thing-in-itself. Its green and gold-embossed cover, with Celtic knot-work writhing and leering from sea to sky, is matched in quality by the finger-feel of the paper. It is simply a lovely book to hold and browse through, as I no doubt repeatedly shall. An excellent work, created with the enthusiasm and skill we have come to expect.

An Essential Index

Tony Fonseca

S. T. JOSHI. *The Horror Fiction Index: An Index to Single-Author Horror Collections, 1808–2010*. Seattle: Sarnath Press, 2023. 733 pp. $25.00 tpb. ISBN: 9798373979931.

In his introduction to *The Horror Fiction Index*, S. T. Joshi explains the need to create an index of single-author horror collections, stating that he has "felt the need for a reference work of this sort for decades." As he notes, such an index of horror and supernatural stories hasn't been published since Donald H. Tuck's three-volume *An Encyclopedia of Science Fiction and Fantasy* (1968–74), which Joshi notes is still useful. But despite its usefulness, Joshi points out that the titles Tuck includes sometimes have little to do with horror or weird fiction. Joshi also notes the existence of E. F. Bleiler's *Guide to Supernatural Fiction* (1983), which he argues is quite valuable. Here as well, however, Joshi points out the text's weakness, namely that Bleiler is "deliberately incomplete even for the volumes he includes." Joshi even compares his vision for his index against the content of the *Internet Speculative Fiction Database* (ISFDB.com), noting that he discovered the site's listings for some volumes were "both incomplete and at times erroneous."

Thus, as Joshi concludes, there is a serious need for a bibliography that fills the gaps that these other resources leave open, and I personally would be hard pressed to think of a more fitting scholar than Joshi to accomplish this task. As he notes, he is a veteran bibliographer in the horror fiction field. He has compiled bibliographies of Lovecraft (Joshi being *the* Lovecraft scholar in just about everyone's estimation), Lord Dunsany, William Hope Hodgson, Clark Ashton Smith, Ambrose Bierce, and Ramsey Campbell. He also has produced *Sixty Years of Arkham House,* which he later revised as *Eighty Years of Arkham House*. When Joshi writes that "I seem to be in a good position to prepare such a volume," he may be making the understatement of the year; very few people are in a better position to prepare such a volume.

As the book's title clearly indicates, the scope of Joshi's index is simple: single-author collections published between 1808 and 2010. Joshi's beginning date is a logical one, as it marks the year that M. G. Lewis's *Romantic Tales* was published. It is not entirely clear why he chooses to end the index with the cut-off year of 2010, which means that it is slightly out-of-date for a 2023 publication; however, that choice does leave room for an updated edition, which many horror fans will be hoping is a project that Joshi is considering. Also a matter of the book's scope is the Joshi's definition of what constitutes a "horror collection." He admits that this determination is "a matter of judgment," adding that he hopes that readers will give him the benefit of the doubt. While this is not the best tactic to explain the scope of an index (or any book, for that matter), the fact that it is Joshi making this statement carries more heft than if it were an indexer who did not have his decades of experience writing about the genre. One could say that if anyone would have a very good sense of what constitutes horror, it would be one of the genre's venerable scholars.

His exclusion criteria begins with a logical exclusion of works that are predominantly in other genres (e.g., science fiction, fantasy [as opposed to dark fantasy], fairy tales, and folklore, unless the last included a collection of horrific fictionalized versions of folklore tales). As for how much of a collection must be devoted to horror, Joshi allows for a generous number, 50 percent; he does, however, exclude short stories published separately as chapbooks or as book club editions (unless the edition is unique in its content). The only exception to the 50 percent rule is with what Joshi calls obvious "borderline cases." Here he gives prominent mainstream examples such as Nathaniel Hawthorne or Gerald Kersh. His other limiter is one of language: he includes only works in the English language, although he makes provisions for works in other languages provided they have appeared in English translation. This is certainly a fair exclusion policy. If Joshi's exclusion criteria do have one weakness, it is that he does not include books published only as ebooks, or ebook editions of print books. Nonetheless, this is understandable, as such inclusion could have made the index unwieldy.

As for the index's structure, Joshi lists volumes alphabetically by author, and then chronologically, with titles all by the same author. As he explains, this allows readers to track original and subsequent publications of a given story, by using his "Index of Story Titles," which are in sequence. For the individual entries, Joshi excludes nonfiction, such as forewords, introductions, afterwords, essays, and poetry, as well as longer fiction, such as novel-length works. He does note every known edition of a volume, but not individual printings of a given edition. Joshi states that his listings of authors' horror fiction collections is complete, except in the case of Edgar Allan Poe. As he notes, Poe's "stories (especially in the twentieth and twenty-first centuries) are all but infinite." He therefore includes only the most significant collections of the past century or so. Joshi also admits that his listing of collections of H. G. Wells's horror fiction may also not be entirely complete.

Both an author's solo work and his or her collaborations are included. Lovecraft presented a bit of a problem, so his "revisions" (Joshi's term) are interfiled with his collections; the posthumous collaborations of Lovecraft and Derleth are listed at the end of the Lovecraft entry. In each entry, Joshi gives basic bibliographic information (i.e., author, title, city of publication, publisher, year) for each collection, which includes a list of all stories in that collection, in the order in which they appear in the collection.

Joshi includes three indexes, an Index of Names, which includes all names not already apparent, such as co-authors, editors, and translators; an Index of Story Titles; and an Index of Collections. These indexes reference not pages but item numbers, which makes it much easier to locate exact editions, to tell at a glance how many books are included per author, and to tell how many books are included in toto, an impressive 3,274 (referencing item numbers over page numbers would also make updates easier, as terms would not have to be reindexed). As a service to researchers (so that they don't have to muddle through so many indexed terms and to take the guesswork out of where troublesome name variations fall alphabetically), minor title variants are not indexed, and names that begin with either "Mc" and "Mac" or "St." are indexed as if they were all "Mac" or "Saint." Joshi states that he "had hoped to include an appendix providing biographical information on the authors, but space restrictions have not permitted."

The ever-gracious Joshi also makes sure to thank the many individuals who have assisted him in providing the tables of contents of books unavailable to him, as well as other important details. The list includes Douglas A. Anderson, s. j. bagley, Michael Darke, Stefan Dziemianowicz, Ross Fletcher, John Linwood Grant, César Guarde-Paz, David Haden, Brian Keene, Roger Lasley, Gavin Lees, Greg Lowney, Bob McGough, Mats Nyholm, Dejan Ognjanovic, Graeme Phillips, Michael Price, David Rigsbey, David E. Schultz, Darrell Schweitzer, Roger Silverstein, Ryan Smith, John C. Tibbetts, and Jamie Turner.

Obviously, researchers and horror fans could and should use the index to determine when the first book publication of a story took place, and in which collection. Scholars and fans with access to a searchable version of the index would be able to find every instance of any given story quickly and efficiently. They would also be able to create a timeline for all publications of a story, although they would have to do slightly more legwork beyond the index to determine if they are looking at a revised version, if one exists. Scholars researching specific authors who are in the index would be able to create a fairly comprehensive bibliography as well, and by the same token, fans of a specific author would be able to find that author's collected works, which is very useful if an individual bibliography does not exist. Of course, some of this information can be found on the Internet, but its accuracy would be questionable until a researcher were to verify it—using refereed and reputable resources (such as this index). Overall, Joshi's index has limited uses, but for researchers and horror fans looking for the information it provides, it will be invaluable.

Howard Days 2023

Bobby Derie

> I can see your point about the preferability of a Cross Plains pilgrimage to a contribution to a Memorial Edition Fund. Undoubtedly—undervaluing his own achievements as he did—good old REH would have considered such a pilgrimage the greater tribute.
>
> —H. P. Lovecraft to E. Hoffmann Price, 11 January 1937
> (*Letters to E. Hoffmann Price & Richard Searight* 274)

It is a little over a thousand miles from my house in Georgia to Robert E. Howard's front door. West of Fort Worth, where they say the West truly begins, the busy highway gives way to a two-lane blacktop that rises over hills and dips into valleys. The dawn breaks and while the countryside grows more arid with every mile, you can see the wildflowers bloom, yellow, pink, and gold. Some miles before Abilene I turned off into a smaller highway, driving past ranches and cows, post oaks and live oaks.

The speed limit drops precipitously, and then drops again. More trees crop up, barbed-wire fences give way to houses . . . and so I arrived, early on a cool and breezy spring morning, in a little town where two rural highways meet.

Cross Plains, Texas. The home of Robert E. Howard.

Thursday, April 27

I have been coming to Howard Days since 2016; first out of curiosity, and later to see friends and visit. As conventions go, Howard Days is a small and intimate affair, never more than a couple of hundred people, some of whom have traveled from halfway across the world to be there. This year, however, they had decided to put me to work: I was to be on three panels, besides my normal business of handing out the free books I had hauled all the way from Georgia.

The convention proper started on Friday, but I had arrived early to check into my hotel—"Where are you staying?" is commonly heard, and unlike conventions held in major or even minor cities, there are no suitable hotels in Cross Plains itself. People stay at hotels and motels in Brownwood, Cisco, and Abilene; at local Airbnbs and in guest rooms, if they're lucky enough to have friends in town with space to spare. Many local Texans simply make a day trip of it, driving in from all over the state.

Brownwood is about forty miles south of Cross Plains, a fair-sized city with a choice of hotels, restaurants, and shops. The historic downtown includes a bookshop built in an old theater called the Intermission, and there are two museums—the Brown County Museum of History, which also offers tours of the Old Jail, and the Martin & Frances Lehnis Railroad Museum. Both are good ways to idle away an hour, but neither knows anything about Robert E. Howard, who had attended high school and one of the local universities, who had first been published in the student papers there and had written about the filling of Lake Brownwood, inspiring a tale called "Wild Water."

A ways past the downtown and the train museum, a small turn-off the road leads into Greenleaf Cemetery. I can't say I was the first that year to park my car and get out on foot, walking down the dusty lane toward the historical marker sign that guides visitors to another kind of marker—because when I turned and stared at the Howard family lot and read the legend there ("They were lovely and pleasant in their lives, and in their death they were not divided."), I saw someone had already placed an old Conan paperback on the stone sill at the foot of the gravestone. The first of many offerings. It's that kind of crowd.

The afternoon found me back in Cross Plains. The docents open the Robert E. Howard House & Museum for a few hours on Thursday afternoon, and the early arrivals filter in and often hang out in the pavilion. The white house with its white picket fence is the same house where Robert E. Howard lived in Cross Plains. The lot that the house sits on now was once part of a suburb, the neighboring houses cleared out by tornado, wildfire, and time to form a large green sward dotted with a few trees that give welcome shade during the summer months.

The local community organization Project Pride bought the house and the land to form Butler Park (the open pavilion being near to where the Butler house stood, the Butlers being Robert E. Howard's nearest neighbors and their children his friends and playmates). Subsequent owners had altered the plan of the house slightly, so that the sleeping porch that once gave some coolness on sweaty summer nights (and where Robert E. Howard died) is now an enclosed hallway, and a small add-on has been turned into the gift shop. A patch of railroad ties and rocks marks the root cellar, which archaeologists from the National Park Service had excavated some years before—a reminder of the history beneath our very feet.

I said my hellos to everyone who was there already and deposited certain books I had brought, mostly signed copies of my *Weird Talers: Essays on Robert E. Howard and Others,* in the gift shop. I did a brief tour of the house, because I like to look at the books rescued from Robert E. Howard's own library, a framed postcard from H. P. Lovecraft, and to look into the cramped little room that had been his. The table was not original, nor the typewriter, though it was an Underwood No. 5 as Howard did use. The hat on the bed had been custom-made by a fan, based on one of Howard's most famous photographs. Sometimes, if you ask nicely, the docents lift the rope and let you sit at that chair, and you can occupy as close as might be experienced the same physical space that Howard himself had . . .

Then it was back outside, to greet old friends and make no ones, to joke and reminisce and get off onto nerdy tangents about all things Robert E. Howard.

Friday, April 28
Normally Howard Days is held in June, often coinciding near the anniversary of Robert E. Howard's death. The summers in Texas, however, have not been getting cooler; it was more than 100° F every day last year, and so this year the event had been moved to the end of April—and, ironically, a cold front moved through. The temperatures during the day were pleasant, but in the early mornings and evenings dropped down into the 50s, with winds sometimes so blustery that it felt cooler still.

My hands were cold as I pulled off the gravel drive and on-to the grass. John Bullard, of the Robert E. Howard Foundation, was already there, and shortly thereafter Arlene Stephenson of Project Pride showed up, to get everything ready. Much of the town joins in Howard Days in one way or another; many of the tables and chairs are borrowed from local churches. I had reserved a dealer's table to set up my free books; this year's product was *The Robert E. Howard Trivia Book,* with 600 questions in six categories, a bit lighthearted. Previous giveaways, all unique to Howard Days, included *The Robert E. Howard Bar Guide, The Robert E. Howard Sampler, Strange Stories of Robert E. Howard & Co.,* and *Cross Plains Pilgrimage.*

Donuts and coffee were set out, and a school bus pulled up. While the town isn't very big, the sites of interest to Howard fans are too scattered about for anything but driving. White-bearded Rusty Burke played tour guide as he showed off the remains of the small communities where the Howards had lived, discussed the history of Cross Plains, and showed off the Pecan Bayou and the bridge made famous from *The Whole Wide World* before the bus rattled back to the pavilion.

By the time the bus was back, the Foundation had set out its table. A nonprofit devoted to publishing Howard's work and continuing his legacy, the Foundation publishes Howard's letters, fiction, and other works; this year it had brought the third volume of Howard's *Collected Letters,* volumes of his *Collected Poetry,* and an exclusive, *The Robert E. Howard Photo Album.* There is no dedicated dealers' room—the handful of dealers who show up every year set out their tables in the sun and wind, with a tent if they've brought one, or in the shade of a tree if they didn't. Small-press publishers such as Rogue Blades and Vanguard, and individual artists, gaming stores, comic shops, and collectors lay out their wares.

Rogue Blades had released a new nonfiction book called *Hither Came Conan,* a collection of essays on all Robert E. Howard's Conan stories—originally a series conceived by Bob Byrne and published on Blackgate.com, but revised and expanded. Jason M. Waltz, publisher and editor, was there in his trademark cowboy hat, shook my hand, and handed me my contributor copy—I had written the essay on "The Phoenix on the Sword," the first Conan story. Throughout the rest of the trip I'd have to pull out my pen to sign other folks' copies, since collecting signatures is another Howard Days tradition.

Around 10 A.M., everything comes alive. The Cross Plains Library opens, showing off its collection of Robert E. Howard's original manuscripts (copies of which are for sale), and original pulps he was published in; gaming sessions are held in a back room. The museum is opened and people move in and out, the Project Pride docents guiding them through the house. The *Cross Plains Review,* the local newspaper and the oldest continuing-operating business in town, opens its doors to show off the old press, the mylar-sleeved newspapers from the 1930s with their announcements of Howard's death, and this year's merchandise (T-shirts, histories of Cross Plains, bookmarks, a printed blanket, etc.). Across the street, the Cross Plains Post Office offers a special Howard-themed postal cancellation stamp, different every year. A line of visitors mail out postcards and letters from Cross Plains just for that, or even ask that the stamp be applied to the books they bought that year.

I visited the post office for a sadder reason: Bill "Indy" Cavalier and his wife Cheryl, who were intimately involved in the organization and running of Howard Days, would not be attending that year. They had arrived on Wednesday feeling under the weather, and a test showed they'd contracted Covid. One can hardly imagine how tough it must have been to jump back in the car and drive home after coming all that way, but it was the right thing to do and Indy deserved all the kudos in the world for doing it. The package I mailed out held a copy of the *Trivia Book,* and a get-well-soon card for Indy and his wife.

The first panel "100 Years of *Weird Tales*" was at 11 at the local Methodist Church, which lent us its parish hall for the occasion. The theme of Howard Days this year was the centenary of *Weird Tales* magazine, whose first issue hit the stand in February 1923, and which had published so much of Howard's work. The guest of honor was John Betancourt of Wildside Press, who had been involved with *Weird Tales* for about twenty-five years, helping to revive the magazine, and joining us was Dierk Guenther from Japan, whose doctoral dissertation had been on Robert E. Howard.

Together, the three of us walked the audience through a weird century, from the earliest beginnings under editor Edwin Baird through the "Golden Age" under Farnsworth Wright and Dorothy McIlwraith, to the various revivals by Moskowitz, Forrest J. Ackermann, Lin Carter, Darrell Schweitzer, Ann VanderMeer, and others right on to the current editor, Jonathan Maberry. I had brought along a box of props to help illustrate some of the phases of the magazine, and Betancourt was especially insightful on the sometimes tumultuous history of the magazine in the last four decades . . . and yet, *Weird Tales* is still with us, the magazine that never dies.

There was a break for lunch, and many including myself tramped back to the pavilion for a free hotdog lunch hosted by Project Pride, where I put more books on the table and directed others not to forget to take a copy. (I've no idea how many folks' first experience of Howard Days involves a short, red-faced man in a black cap and a strange T-shirt asking if they've gotten their free book yet, but probably dozens at this point. Possibly hundreds.) The cake offered up for dessert had been printed with the cover of the first issue of *Weird Tales*. Then it was back to the Methodist church for the second panel.

"The 3 Musketeers of *Weird Tales*" was a discussion of Robert E. Howard, H. P. Lovecraft, and Clark Ashton Smith; the other panelists were Mark Finn (author of *Blood & Thunder: The Life & Art of Robert E. Howard*) and Jeff Shanks (co-editor of *The Unique Legacy of Weird Tales: The Evolution of Modern Fantasy & Horror*). The discussion focused mainly on how *Weird Tales* had defined those three titans of fantasy, and how they in turn had defined *Weird Tales*. I even managed to sneak in a brief mention of Seabury Quinn, who was the most popular author at *Weird Tales* from 1923 to 1954, although overshadowed by Lovecraft, Howard, and Smith today.

As we wrapped up, the Glenn Lord Symposium stepped into the vacant chairs. Like the Armitage Symposium at NecronomiCon Providence, this was a more scholarly presentation. Jason Ray Carney (author of *Weird Tales of Modernity:*

The Ephemerality of the Ordinary in the Stories of Robert E. Howard, Clark Ashton Smith and H. P. Lovecraft and co-editor of *The Dark Man: Journal of Robert E. Howard and Pulp Studies*) acted as moderator for the three presenters who took turns presenting their papers: Dierk Guenther, with a discussion on racism in Howard's "The Vale of Lost Women"; Brian Murphy (author of *Flame and Crimson: A History of Sword and Sorcery*) analyzing Howard as an author writing in a closed frontier; and Howard scholar Will Oliver, who had done quantitative research on a series of 1930s interviews in oil boom towns in Texas to see whether they corroborated Howard's own accounts of the Cross Plains Oil Boom.

Immediately after that, Rusty Burke took charge of the microphone and we segued into the Robert E. Howard Foundation Awards ceremony. These awards are given every year, voted on by the members of the Foundation, as part of the Foundation's mission to promote the study of Howard's life and works, and to encourage his creative legacy as well, by recognizing fiction writers and artists working in a Howardian vein. The full list of winners can be found at rehfoundation.org/winners-of-the-2023-rehf-awards/ but special mention must go to Fred Blosser, who was given the lifetime achievement award—the Black Circle. Blosser's essays on Howard in the pages of *Savage Sword of Conan* in the 1970s had been the starting point for many Howard scholars alive today, and he is still publishing in the 2020s, which is phenomenal.

I missed an informal panel on "Howard's Women" held by Janice Schange with Aurelia Wilder, Libby Sharpe, and Stephani Childress at the Cottonwood Coffee Shop; the wind had ripped through the dealer's area in a particularly sharp gust during the panels and knocked aside tents and books, though fortunately someone had saved mine before they were scattered all over creation. Even as we stood there in the pavilion, we could feel the temperature drop and the wind not letting up a bit . . . but as the sun moved toward the western horizon, we made our way to the Baptist church for the banquet and the silent auction.

The banquet is the only part of Howard Days that requires money or signing up in advance; anyone can roll up into town on the day of and walk through the museum and attend the panels for free, but you need to buy a ticket for the banquet, and since there are only so many seats, they can go fast. The banquet was sold out this year, which is not uncommon, but because of the date or the weather several people who had bought tickets couldn't show, and everyone who wanted to managed to get in.

The silent auction is a personal favorite of the Howard Days tradition; attendees (including myself) mail or bring in all sorts of donations, from old pulp magazines and comics to rare Howard-related books and memorabilia. Pieces of the Howard House, removed during restorations, have been auctioned off there, and original artwork, signed books, letters from Howard's friends, foreign-language books and comics, and all manner of things—and they are priced to move, much below what similar articles would fetch online through eBay or the like. The only limit at the auction is that sales have to be conducted by cash or check, as they aren't set up to take credit cards or mobile payment schemes.

Before we dug into our chicken-fried steak and double-baked mashed potatoes, there was the normal business to attend to: brief speeches and Rusty Burke on behalf of the Foundation thanking everyone for making this possible, the awarding of a scholarship to a Cross Plains student on her way to college, and then the guest of honor took the stand. John Gregory Betancourt was modest and self-effacing, but his efforts in publishing had kept the lights on at *Weird Tales,* he was friends with many prominent writers, editors, and publishers, and his story of how he had gotten his start—and the Conan novel he had almost written—were well received by all.

As the banquet wound down and the auction results came in, the weather outside had gotten colder, and the wind had not abated. It was in the 50s and dropping, and there was a mist in the air. Normally at this point, a few dedicated attendees would brave the mosquitos and head to the lot at the back of the Ice House, where Robert E. Howard had once boxed, but given the weather the Fists at the Ice House panel was moved to the Methodist church. There, Mark Finn, Jeff Shanks, and Chris Gruber (*Fist of Iron,* the collected boxing stories of Robert E. Howard) recited passages from Howard's boxing yarns and talked about what boxing meant to him. It was a good panel, but lacked something as we could not be on the "hallowed ground" behind the Ice House this year.

It was late and dark by the time I got back to the pavilion. The fellowship can last into the early hours of the morning, as the beer and whiskey starts to flow, but it was too cold and windy for even the most devoted of us to endure for long. A half-hour or so was my limit, and well before midnight I was back on the road to Brownwood to catch a few hours of sleep.

Saturday, April 29
Dawn caught me on my way back to Cross Plains. Saturday tends to be crowded, since all the day-trippers come in for the weekend, and just down the road at Treadway Park the Cross Plains Spring Fling Festival was starting up. Along with the other dealers, I set my table back up and stacked the books high as a bulwark against the wind, which was less breezy than yesterday. I had brought 200 copies of the *Trivia Book* to give away and was hoping not to take any home. Most of the dealers were eager to offload their remaining stock as well.

Down on Main Street, the crowd gathered to follow Rusty Burke on the walking tour. This was the counterpart to yesterday's bus tour, showing folks all the sights they could see propelled by their own two legs, including the boarding house where Novalyne Price had stayed when she was dating Robert E. Howard in 1934–36. As the tour wrapped up, the pavilion began to fill up and there was time for conversation and catching up with folks I hadn't seen in a year or more.

The first panel, and the last for which I was responsible, was "Robert E. Howard and *Weird Tales*." John Betancourt acted as moderator, pitching questions to myself and Patrice Louinet of France (a leading Howard scholar who earned a doctorate from the Sorbonne about Robert E. Howard, author of *The Howard Guide,* etc.) about Howard's relationship with *Weird Tales*. It was a good panel; Patrice and I had discussed matters such as *Strange Stories* (the third magazine to *Weird Tales* and *Oriental Stories* that never quite came to fruition) previously in private, but now got to talk about them openly in front of an audience, and we were able to cover a lot of ground in Howard's career, from his first story "Spear and Fang" to the mystery of why he didn't have a larger posthumous presence in the magazine.

After the break for lunch, where I had my annual soft-serve ice cream cone at the local Dairy Queen, we were back in the Methodist church for the final panel. "The Art of *Weird Tales*" had an excellent lineup—J. David Spurlock (*The Alluring Art of Margaret Brundage: Queen of Pulp Pin-Up Art,* etc.), Michael Tierney (*The Robert E. Howard Art Chronology*), and Dennis McHaney (*Robert E. Howard and* Weird Tales, *Robert E. Howard in the Pulps,* etc.) talked about the art and artists through the last century of *Weird Tales*. Fortunately, the church was set up with a screen so the audience could actually see the art being discussed.

The last formal presentation was the annual "What's New with Robert E. Howard" panel, with Paul Herman and Rusty Burke discussing new and upcoming publishing projects as far as books, comics, games, etc. Yet the real show-stopper was at the end, when Herman went into a side-room and brought forth an old oak table, setting it up on the table at the front of the room so that everyone could see it—and Paul Herman told the story.

It was Robert E. Howard's writing table.

After the death of Robert and his mother in 1936, Dr. Isaac M. Howard had given away much of the furniture to neighbors. Robert's writing table from his room had been disposed of this way, and the woman who received it had cut the legs short to serve as a coffee table. It had remained with that family after the woman's death, and Herman had kept track of it all through the years . . . until the family finally decided to part with it. The Robert E. Howard Foundation announced its intention to have the table professionally restored and installed in Robert's room at the museum.

A magic moment, and the crowd gathered around to lay their hands on the "True Table," tongues firmly in cheek and yet . . . we were joking and not joking. This was what we had come here for, after all. To connect with Robert E. Howard in this place, at this time. There is nowhere else in the world where you could have that kind of fleeting, intimate connection with the past—and no other time when you can share that kind of moment with other people who understand exactly what it means, because they're there for the same reason.

In the afternoons in the pavilion, as the sun goes down in the west, the shadows shift and the crowd tends to shift with it. The dealers put up their tables. The talk gets a little louder. A rogue panel on the rebirth of sword-&-sorcery broke out, though I didn't hear much of it as Rusty Burke was giving a tour of the grounds of the house, showing off the historic markers, describing how the house had been when he had first seen it, and how it had been in Howard's time. Rusty had been part of that first group of fans to make the pilgrimage to Cross Plains, and he works hard to share his knowledge and appreciation for what has been built here . . . a community that supports and welcomes Howard fans, and their most famous former resident.

The Saturday night barbecue is our last shared meal. Jack and Barbara Baum funded it this year, and it is a simple meal of brisket and potato salad, beans and bread, with cookies for dessert. The drinks come out of an old Army cooler in the corner, which from time to time folks top up with ice, bottled water, soda, and often beer as we get closer to evening. In other years, when the heat and humidity sucks the moisture out of you, the cooler is a lifesaver; in the coolness of that Saturday night, it was simply refreshing to plunge a hand down into icy water and come up with a drink.

As the evening draws in, the crowd gathers on the porch to recite poetry. Everyone is welcome, and some are volunteered. Robert E. Howard's poem "Cimmeria" is often read in as many languages as there are speakers, from Italian to Japanese, Latin to Gaelic. When they are done, and the darkness closes in, the pavilion becomes the centerpiece . . . people laugh, drink, recite poetry, ask trivia questions; gamers roll dice, podcasts are recorded. Ben Frieberg, who diligently records all the panels and will upload them to YouTube, breaks out his homemade ice cream. Final gifts are made, and one by one the crowd melts away. Goodbyes can take half an hour or more to say, as no one wishes to miss saying goodbye to anyone else.

Yet all good things must end, and the road from Cross Plains stretches as long back to Georgia as it does getting there. With the car a couple of hundred books lighter, I left them there not far from midnight. It would be a long year before I would see any of them again.

Classics from a Contemporary

The joey Zone

ALLEN KOSZOWSKI, *Dreams from The Dark Side*. Introduction by Ramsey Campbell. Lakewood, CO: Centipede Press, 2023. 568 pp. $70.00 hc. ISBN: 9781613473207.

With its crimson-lit phantasmagorical dust jacket and matching top edge–painted signatures, this long overdue collection is a veritable visual Baedeker to the borderlands of horror and science fantasy, a fitting tribute to an artist who is a continual and vital inspiration to us all.

In 1986, one eye winked at me, the other was an empty socket. Out of the sentient stippled decay in the foreground of the cover to Joe Lansdale's *Dead in the West,* this Old School Finlayesque approach by the illustrator, Allen Koszowski, definitely was not lazy art, being impressive in its myriad multi-dot universe.

I still have the T-shirt with a design by Allen that was also the cover of the Program Guide for the second Necro-nomiCon in 1995, in those epochs held in Danvers, Massachusetts. Various monstrosities burrow through a copy of Alhazred's holy writ and lurk behind the *Revelations of Glaaki*. There was an interior illustration by Koszowski for Guest of Honor Ramsey Campbell—they go way back. Meanwhile, yours truly got a Days Pass for working as a "go-fer" (some call that a "minion" nowadays) and had the "rough" assignment of hanging out and assisting at the dealers' room—eternal thanks to Marc Michaud for laying the gease upon a humble scrivener!

Allen is one of the Three Musketeers of Necronomicon Press, which includes Jason Eckhardt and Robert Knox. Notable from that imprint was the cover he did for Josef Janzoon's *Final Diary Entry of Kees Huitgens* (1995). It is a case of him successfully embracing the Surreal akin to his publishing mate Knox. Koszowski won the 2002 World Fantasy

Award, the Gahan Wilson–designed Howard. A year later he himself was a GoH at World Fantasy and for that event did a notable portrait of Jack Williamson with his creations April Bell, Barbee in his true Smilodon form, and others, finally seeing print in this Centipede collection.

In 2013, as the art editor of the Program Guide for NecronomiCon Providence (The Next Generation), I had the honor of curating a new illustration of Wilbur Whateley by Allen Koszowski for publication.

*****

The first 25 pages of this book showcase portraits done for the single-author collections John Pelan edited under the Midnight House and Darkside Press imprints. Thanks to Allen, this reviewer will be looking up work by Dick Donovan, Vivian Meik, and others. After these is the portrait of Lee Brown Coye we were proud to publish here first (*Dead Reckonings* No. 32). Wrapping up this section is the dust jacket for one of the works Koszowski justly rates among his best, for S. T. Joshi's *Sixty Years of Arkham House* (Arkham House, 1999), depicting the many tomes billowing out of that seminal eerie edifice.

A back cover, superior to the fine front cover (also by Allen) in its striking simplicity, was that for James Van Hise's *Stephen King and Clive Barker: The Illustrated Guide 2* (1991): a fanged skull has each writer in an eye socket's "reflection"—they being the eyes envisioning the macabre. Colored over in red upon publication, the detail shewn here is ever more evident. One of the standout pieces in this book is Koszowski's illustration for "Queen of the Black Coast," originally appearing in Van Hise's *Fantastic Worlds of Robert E. Howard* (1997). While the original printing of it in that volume was much larger, the range of grays done on coquille paper shows up in greater detail here due to Centipede Press' impeccable production values. A Howard fan should have this book on the shelf for this image alone!

Included in this volume is one of this writer's favorite pieces by the artist, the cover for Hippocampus Press' edition of Herbert Gorman's 1927 novel *A Place Called Dagon* (2000). There is a whole series in *Dreams* featuring depictions of Cthulhu ITself (fitting)—the recent cover for *Allen K.'s Inhuman* #5 giving that Great Old One the true cyclopean dimensions.

Through the Trapezohedron Glass: the cover for *Crypt of Cthulhu* #22 (Necronomicon Press, Roodmas 1984) here with an example Allen's great hand-drawn lettering.

The early issues of the fanzine *Midnight Marquee* boasted some of Allen's finest portraiture of film icons of fear and fantasti-film, such as that of Rondo Hatton from #37, its 25th Anniversary Issue. Another James Van Hise book was *Serial Adventures* (1990), presenting a superb wraparound cover featuring—in Glorious Black & White!—Lewis Wilson's Batman, Victor Jory's Shadow, The Spider, etc. Although the art is printed in this collection, I need to get the original book now as well—Koszowski Art *is* that good. Included in *Dreams* are a number of images seeing publication for the first time, a selling point if one was needed. Some feature depictions by Allen of the most interesting people with the most . . . worm-eaten complexions. That said, this is not a fully annotated *catalogue raisonné:* a look at the Internet Speculative Fiction Database (which in itself is incomplete!) proves that to be a production still many reproductions away from. An example of a piece missing in action is S. T. Joshi depicted in periwigged pastiche (may he always deport himself so!) of Virgil Finlay's famous Lovecraft portrait on the cover of *Classics and Contemporaries* (Hippocampus Press, 2009). But anon for that. Thanks to The Artist himself for providing Credit Where Due on some of these pieces. "But I have been turning out a bunch of stuff . . . I can't stop!"

More classics assuredly to come from someone who—may he long remain our contemporary!

Ramsey's Rant:
Gidget Goes Yog-Sothoth

Ramsey Campbell

I still recall the frissons I experienced in my youth on encountering Lovecraftian references in the wild. Hearing them spoken seemed to have a special power, and I relished the mentions of the Necronomicon and Cthulhu in Corman's film *The Haunted Palace,* along with the allusion to Azathoth in Harvey Hart's *Dark Intruder* (written by Barré Lyndon, the last of his several scripts of the macabre and fantastic). A film whose poster boasted Lovecraft's name promised much, and I was eager to catch *The Dunwich Horror* at the cinema, only to find the British censor had shorn it (sometimes very visibly) of four minutes. The recent Arrow Blu-ray has let me reappraise the film in terms of how it was intended to appear.

After an unusually understated prologue that drops hints to the alert viewer, showing Lavinia Whateley led from her bedroom to give birth somewhere unspecified, the credits sequence delivers a bunch of blows to Lovecraftian expectations. The imagery depicts a standard horned demon—admittedly a big one—gobbling up a victim, and top billing goes to Sandra Dee. While she recently acted in her finest film, *Imitation of Life,* Douglas Sirk still drew upon her teenage screen persona, which seems so thoroughly established that American-International may well have cast her in *The Dunwich Horror* as the latest of their bids to woo a youthful audience, though she saw the film as her bid to gain onscreen adulthood. She plays Nancy Wagner, a Miskatonic University student trusted with restoring the *Necronomicon* (a copy so pristine we might assume it has been rebound) to its glass case. She's immediately approached by Wilbur Whateley (Dean Stockwell). Is Stockwell's version of him excessively humanised? I find that when or if the initial disappointment wears off, the quiet hypnotic charm with which he wins Nancy over does seem to suggest darker qualities held in check, an impression perhaps underpinned these days by memories of his quintessentially strange turn in *Blue Velvet*. In the Whateley role he's surely preferable to Peter Fonda, the initial choice, presumably intended as one of the film's attempts to evoke the psychedelic. Once he starts reading from the *Necronomicon* it's clear Stockwell means to treat the Lovecraftian elements with due respect, even if the text has been simplified (less a King James version than a Good News Necronomicon). Nancy drives him forty miles to Dunwich, where the sight of Wilbur turns a petrol pump attendant taciturn (one of a number of effectively understated scenes). Although Daniel Haller has relinquished designing sets to take up direction, the Victorian interior of the Whateley house is impressively ornate, and he withholds a high angle to display to greatest effect how an occult sign has been worked into the décor, prefiguring Kubrick's version of the Overlook Hotel.

Wilbur tricks Nancy into staying overnight and spikes her cup of tea. The drug assails her with visions of an erotic chase and what appears to be a sexual initiation, which perhaps prepares her for the climactic ritual (though Sandra Dee refused to play the latter scene nude as written, and we may wonder how comfortable she was with the hippyish nakedness the pursuers display in her hallucination). The sequence may also be seen as one of the film's attempts to woo the turned-on generation, and Stockwell plays the act of drugging the drink as a solemn ritual (the kind of sombrely serious rite the preamble to getting high often was in those days). A striking moment has her elude the chase by running straight into the room she's sleeping in (Lavinia's old bedroom), undermining our sense of where reality ends.

Next day brings Nancy's friend Elizabeth (Donna Bacala) and Professor Henry Armitage (Ed Begley) in search of her. The screenplay deftly intertwines their investigation of Dunwich and the Whateleys with Nancy's developing relationship. The structural care anticipates Curtis Hanson's celebrated adaptation of *LA Confidential,* but here he's only one of three credited screenwriters; perhaps that's why the narrative keeps being invaded by the inexplicable if not the haphazard (for instance, the way Nancy's orgiastic vision suggests a cult, although Wilbur is as solitary as his literary prototype). The film develops a tension between classical narrative and contemporary trippiness, and perhaps this contrast can be read short-hand for the intrusion of Lovecraftian chaos into the mundane.

As the film edges towards revelation the imagery grows either random or obliquely evocative, possibly both. The Devil's Hopyard proves to be a variously weird promontory over-looking the sea. The ceremony for which it is the site conflates a fertility ritual with the summoning of Lovecraft's Old Ones, a notion underlying the original tale. While reviving it Wilbur makes Crowley's trademark gesture, one instance of the film's eclectic approach to the occult, which brings in tarot cards as well. Can this be seen as consistent with Lovecraft? Surely the difference is that he sought to integrate received elements into his imaginative vision, generally interpreting them in its terms, whereas the film seems to introduce them randomly in the hope they'll prove evocative. If they do, it's thanks to Stockwell's committed performance.

The film has yet to deal with its central secret—Wilbur's hidden brother. At intervals he's been signified by massive restlessness in the attic (the film's domestic version of Lovecraft's barn). The more a sense of horror beyond a door is built up, the harder it may be to deliver a satisfactory payoff. For instance, David Greene's *The Shuttered Room* hardly tries, not even bothering with the Lovecraftian. Haller's previous Lovecraft film—*Die, Monster, Die!*—exhibited some impressive mutations, but this time his solution is subliminal, rather in the way we're restricted to monstrous glimpses of the mutated Freda Jackson in the earlier film: when Elizabeth opens the attic door in search of Nancy both her attacker and the attack challenge our perceptions with a psychedelic riot of solarised images. The scene and subsequent manifestations feel effectively restrained compared to the zingy lightshows occult confrontations apparently demand these days (perhaps rooted in the magical duel in Corman's *The Raven,* but that was the climax of a comedy). As unknowable in its motivations as in its form, the occupant then returns to the attic.

The death of Wilbur's grandfather (authoritatively played

by Sam Jaffe) brings the tarot to his funeral. Here as elsewhere Stockwell's performance is quietly persuasive, so that the invasion of his graveside rite by local objectors comes across as a real intrusion; perhaps, like Nancy, we've succumbed to his seductiveness. Lavinia dies in an asylum, where her vision seems to have been solarised by her occult impregnation or else the birth of Wilbur and his brother. Wilbur involves an entranced Nancy in a ritual to release his sibling, at which point the film's structure falters. In the original story the brother breaks loose because no family is left to tend it, but here its rampage seems wholly unrelated to Wilbur's reason for summoning it (even if we assume that simply opening the attic door would prove as fatal to him as it was to Elizabeth). Its emergence from the attic causes the conflagration Corman normally reserved for the coda, but here we have another reel to go. As Wilbur continues his grave gentle ritual (heavily and audibly cut at the time by the censor on the original British release), the brother picks off random villagers in a colourful and raucous if unspecified fashion while Armitage and the local doctor (Lloyd Bochner) drive to the rescue. An occult duel between Wilbur and the professor ends in lightning, and we're afforded a glimpse of the inhuman brother. If it appears more Gorgonian than Lovecraftian, perhaps we may take this as shorthand for an entity that should not be looked upon. In any case, the sharp-eyed viewer should spot evidence of its relationship to Wilbur, an unexpected acknowledgment of Lovecraft's final revelation. Is Armitage's declaration that the father was "not of this earth" a witty nod to Corman? Cartoonish though it is, the final image recalls both *Rosemary's Baby* and *2001,* thus conflating the occult and the cosmic. In sum, *The Dunwich Horror* is a film whose ideas may haunt the mind, even if we miss the lost possibility of a Lovecraftian movie directed by Mario Bava (the original proposal).

The Arrow Blu-ray offers a fine transfer of the previously unreleased complete version, as established by Steve Bissette and Stephen Laws in a wide-ranging conversation on the disc. Other extras include a trailer, an informative if eccentric commentary track by Guy Adams and Alexandra Benedict (creators of the *Arkham County* audio drama), and a contextualisation of the film by Ruthanna (*Innsmouth Legacy*) Emrys. At 15:55 into her contribution, a disembodied voice utters an unidentifiable word behind her, which she assures me she didn't hear at the time. Has she or some aspect of the disc invoked an uncanny intruder? By all means investigate the Arrow release. It may contain occult secrets yet to manifest themselves on the world.

Dark Nights of the Soul: Part I

Michael D. Miller

MATT CARDIN. *Journals, Volume 1: 1993–2001*. Seattle: Sarnath Press, 2022. 337 pp. $16.95 tpb. ISBN: 979-8357810830

> The purpose of the world is for you to transcend it.
> —Eckhart Tolle

Sarnath Press has expanded its publication output with Matt Cardin's *Journals, Volume 1: 1993–2001* being the latest offering. Originally a press solely handling part of the voluminous output of weird fiction scholar, editor, anthologist, and H. P. Lovecraft expert S. T. Joshi, the publisher now offers the Ambrose Bierce's *Collected Essays and Journalism* (edited by Joshi and David E. Schultz) and the journals of Matt Cardin, with more in the works. Sarnath, the name, is interesting to many readers as it is a place name setting in Lovecraft's fiction, and a city in India, where, according to some legends, Buddha was born.

Matt Cardin is certainly in perfect company at Sarnath Press, having two recent publications of note with Hippocampus Press, the short story collection *To Rouse Leviathan* (2019), which I reviewed in *Dead Reckonings* No. 27, and the collection of essays on horror, film, and philosophy, *What the Daemon Said* (2022). Beyond these, Cardin is an academic who has taught religious studies and has been involved in the proliferation of the work of Thomas Ligotti, editing *Born to Fear: Interviews with Thomas Ligotti* (2014), all while serving as co-editor of the journal *Vastarien,* a journal of "critical study and creative response to the corpus of Thomas Ligotti as well as associated authors and ideas." Cardin has also been sharing his philosophical work on social media for years, through his long-running blog *The Teeming Brain* (now defunct), his new blog newsletter *Living into the Dark* and the published instructional manual *A Course in Demonic Creativity: A Writer's Guide to the Inner Genius*. All this makes the publication of a personal journal seemingly warranted.

Established writers sharing their personal thoughts and philosophies of life and the subject of writing: a very verdant field that is often overlooked. Perhaps those reflections are too academic or not financially profitable enough to encourage a greater awareness and market of such personal writing. Yet there are a number of prominent writers whose ideas and commentary I enjoy more than their fictional output, Stephen King and Harlan Ellison being two of them. Then there are those select few writers whose fiction, personal philosophies, and ideas generating them are equally rewarding as seen in such masters of the form as H. P. Lovecraft or Thomas Ligotti. Matt Cardin is proving to be among the Elysium of the latter. This is important because it means the work is real, created from a suffering mind, and honed ritually by the writer in daily life. Thus, Cardin's output is not merely written for a sale, or entertainment, or one's personal amusement, but as a continual rethinking of an often painful philosophical worldview. That should be enough to encourage obtaining these journals and reading them, but let us have a further look.

The philosophical exegesis in the journals is a distillation of traditional Western philosophy from Aristotle to Nietzsche with Eastern philosophy, purified in a cauldron of Lovecraftian cosmicism and Ligottian pessimism. Imbued in the mix is the ever-present influence of religion, Christianity in particular (a personal matter for Matt Cardin through the First Christian Church), into the process of writing. This process is examined and identified to be what Cardin refers to as "the demon muse," a guardian angel, or, in the Western Hermetic/Crowleyan tradition, "the holy guardian angel" or true self. I identified and named this process "epistemological alchemy" in my review of *To Rouse Leviathan*. Cardin's dealings and suffering through this process are chronicled over a nine-year period in Volume 1.

What makes these journals not simply "a semi-scholarly attitude of objectivity" layered against obvious subjective writings is Cardin's willingness to face vulnerability. The act of writing is meant to be vulnerable. Writers are vulnerable when crafting fiction, when writing reviews, and most certainly when publishing the personal journals of their intimate psyche. It is worth noting that Cardin tried this twice before—and failed; what we are reading is the third incarnation of that agency. Cardin begins with some early struggles against sleep paralysis attacks leading to hypnagogic visions; some of the episodes recall the early experiences Lovecraft had with dream realities and night-gaunts, forming a connection to that evocative trait common to many writers of the horror genre. Cardin remains very clear that this is about an inner life, an "inner autobiography" standing in context with an external one. He expresses this theme as:

> to search for a spiritual philosophical answer to the riddle of life, as informed and abetted by a profusion of books, authors, philosophers, and sages, many of whom I only partly or sometimes flat-out wrongly understood as I appropriated them for my own unconscious ends, using them as fodder to think the thoughts, feel the feelings, and move philosophically and spiritually in the directions that I was interiorly programmed to move.

Interestingly, we as readers might already be compelled to confront such considerations, if unconsciously, but the journals make us much more aware of that compulsion. That is a jarring notion, but Cardin makes this realization okay because we can recognize it, struggle, process, and move on.

While it is impossible to highlight every significant entry from a journal of this length, a few highly impressive entries are 9/25/98, when Cardin learns his role in *Ligotti Online;* 10/8/98, where he struggles with the assumption that we really don't understand what we read, but just convince ourselves that we do; and 12/17/98, a parallel of the Christian "born again" principle of freeing oneself from sin with the Zen/Taoist idea of the inability to attain enlightenment. The concluding month of August 2001 details a number of plot-germs and writing ideas, some becoming finished stories, but many remaining unused. As an added finality Matt leaves us with "having presently reached what feels like the end of the line as a fiction writer."

I highly recommend these journals and hope to see the remaining volumes published for one reason above all others: Matt dwells in those moments where we question what we do and often wrestle with the thought of abandoning the work. The nihilism of the self is treated with the most existential form of writer's block therapy and emerges on the other side, with a fresh understanding to continue what we do. In that sense, for writers truly embracing the tough questions and doubt of the inner world, Matt Cardin lights a path in all that dark.

[N.B. Volume 2 of Cardin's *Journals* will be published later this year.]

An Introduction to the Horror Films of Paul Wendkos

Clark Tucker

During a career that spanned forty years and dozens of theatrical features, television episodes, and made-for-TV films, Paul Wendkos (1925–2009) always infused his work with distinctive stylistic verve, excellent direction of actors—among those he directed to outstanding performances are Lloyd Bridges, Lesley Ann Warren, Rip Torn, Cecily Tyson, and John Heard—and a variety of subject matter that can give the Wendkos diver serious whiplash.

Beginning with the independently produced David Goodis film adaptation *The Burglar* (1957), starring Dan Duryea and Jane Mansfield, Wendkos's range of work includes the first three films in the popular Gidget series with Sandra Dee; compelling World War II dramas such as *Battle of the Coral Sea* (1959), with Cliff Robertson; the evangelical drama *Angel Baby* (1961), starring a young Burt Reynolds; episodic television directing for some of the era's most popular series, including *The Untouchables* (1959–63) and *The Naked City* (1958–63); and a myriad of dynamic television films such as *The Death of Richie* (1977), with Robbie Benson and Ben Gazzara.

While the entirety of his output is worth one's time and focus, Wendkos's work in the horror genre, be it a film intended for the silver screen or television, represents a major body of achievement in the genre, coupling stylistic verve and visual invention with his gifts for the direction of actors. In recent years, as a plethora of his work has become available on platforms such as YouTube and Amazon Prime in addition to remastered Blu-ray releases, Wendkos's stature as a pioneering horror and suspense filmmaker can be better studied and appreciated in totality than ever before. I have chosen to write about three features in order to convey what I feel to be the innovative and formal character of Wendkos's particular cinematic voice, but he produced so much that the following must ultimately be taken as an introduction.

Originally broadcast in March 1969 on NBC, *Fear No Evil* is both Wendkos's first TV movie and his debut in the horror genre. *Fear No Evil* is centered around David Sorel (Louis Jourdan), a psychiatrist specializing in patients haunted by paranormal visions. He begins treating Barbara (Lynda Day), who has begun seeing the ghost of her fiancé Paul (Bradford Dillman), after his death during an accident in their antique car.

Wendkos's bravura stylizations hurl the viewer into the story with the very first shot: a nearly upside-down image of Paul, wracked and tortured (by what?) escaping from somewhere quickly and running down a street late at night. The edges of the frame have a glossy, dreamlike blur. The delirium evoked by the filmmaking recalls the Orson Welles of *Touch of Evil,* though rendered here in blazing colors whose candy sheen and rich textures become augmented greatly by the recent HD transfer by Kino.

Shots and passages throughout the film are consistently audacious. Wendkos's aesthetic is what one might call "cocktail lounge occult," draping costumes and bouffant hairstyles of the day with shadows and shafts of ominous light. It is worth noting that the interiors in every Wendkos work are often shrouded in a dimness that feels like the outward manifestation of narrative threat. Following Paul's death, there is a haunting, psychedelic shot in which the mirror Barbara is looking into—a mirror purchased by Paul earlier in the film—dissolves into a long corridor and Paul's image appears in a wash as a blood-red silhouette. It is a moment that feels reminiscent of German expressionist cinema at its strongest, strangest, and most sinister. Sorel's meeting with a mutual friend of questionable loyalties (Carroll O'Connor) in a darkened laboratory where a crimson laser is being demonstrated casts them into near abstraction and complements the lurid color splash of Italian Giallo films such as Mario Bava's *Blood and Black Lace* (1964).

As a distraught Barbara is comforted by her untrustworthy mother-in-law outside the family mansion at night, the windswept branches above cast their anguished faces in flickers of strobe-like assault. The climax, where the entire malevolent plot of the supernatural conspiracy is revealed, is a tour de force of cinematic horror, as the camera spirals around cultists in ceremonial masks chanting the name of their demon god and a psychedelic maelstrom sucks Barbara into the mirror as Sorel desperately follows her. A simply arresting passage returns the characters and viewers to the site of Paul's last moments, only now the image is rendered in a dislocating negative effect as Sorel, deposited in the zone of the fatal moment, pulls Barbara away from the intended union with a ghastly body-jumping entity, speaking to her in telepathic voice-over.

Perhaps Wendkos's most notable and highest profile engagement with the supernatural comes in the 1971 body-stealing (as opposed to demonic possession) theatrical release *The Mephisto Waltz,* based on the novel by Fred Mustard Stewart and produced by television's high-powered Quinn Martin, for whom Wendkos directed numerous series episodes. A married couple, frustrated concert pianist turned music journalist Myles Clarkson and his wife Paula (Alan Alda and Jacqueline Bisset), living hand-to-mouth with their small daughter, fall into the snare of a wealthy and world-famous pianist, Ely Duncan (Curd Jurgens). Duncan is on the brink of succumbing to a terminal illness, and the couple discovers all too late its role in a devious occult conspiracy. By molding a mask of the husband's face, Duncan is able to transfer his aging soul into the spry body of Clarkson. The newly "deceased" master leaves a generous portion of his estate to his mentee. Despite the newfound wealth, Paula is chilled by her spouse's cruel and forbidding new manner (at Duncan's "funeral" after her sarcastic comment on his coterie's prayer rituals, he snaps at her to respect other people's religious beliefs) and begins to investigate.

This concept is admittedly nothing too groundbreaking and reminiscent of tales such as Walter de la Mare's *The Return* and H. P. Lovecraft's "The Thing on the Doorstep" as well as the recent mega-successful novel and film of *Rosemary's Baby* (1967 and 1968, respectively). And yet, Wendkos produces a standout horror film of the 1970s.

A costume party at Duncan's vast estate becomes a Boschian nightmare of cackling animal masks worn by elite revelers (plus the shocking reverse, a human mask worn by Duncan's vicious watchdog); Wendkos's career-long thematic interest in dislocation is given full flower as his restless camera cranes and dips into skewed angles metaphorically visualizing the bottom falling out of their lives. Fisheye lenses curve the frame, trapping the characters in a clammy terror that mummifies their perceptions. Paula starts encountering the nefarious Duncan in vivid dreams, wandering through a house transformed into a lonely terminal of ghostly illumination and overgrown cobwebs. Bisset is more or less asked to carry the last half of the film and does a superb job, though Alda excels playing essentially two roles; and Barbara Perkins, as Duncan's equally sinister daughter Roxanne, matches evil with a knowing, decadent sensuality, suggesting perhaps Paula's own repressed desires.

Complementing the onslaught of dread are tricky moral questions raised by the narrative element of body transference. Is Myles allowing his consciousness to be forfeited in order to find the acclaim and fortune that always dodged him? Despite what she uncovers, Paula is still very attracted to Myles—or is it a figure of Duncan's stature currently steering his body that leads her into a truly unconventional climactic decision?

One of Wendkos's better-known works is *The Legend of Lizzie Borden* (1975), a true-crime study of the arrest and trial in the 1890s of the infamous woman acquitted of the brutal ax murders of her father and stepmother yet remembered today, from numerous films and playground songs, as a wicked boogeywoman. Shocking fans of her wholesome *Bewitched* role, Elizabeth Montgomery plays Borden, distraught the day after the crimes, maintaining her innocence throughout the heated and controversial trial, convincing *us* through layers of thespianism that she is entirely blameless.

The film is densely constructed, taking us into flashbacks both expounded in the courtroom by relatives and friends of the family as well as private memories of the flawed domestic situation. Doted on by her mortician father and locked in a rivalry with her stepmother that worsened as Lizzie stayed with them into her thirties, the film constructs a tapestry of long-held familial resentments and potential abuse lurking around the edges of Borden's rosy patriarchal memories. Certain moments and images, such as the child Lizzie accidentally pulling an embalming tube that sends a gout of blood spattering through her dad's workroom, repeat with talismanic significance, similar to shots in the experimental thrillers of Nicholas Roeg and Donald Cammell.

Wendkos weaves complex strands of perception, memory, and a kind of psychic confession as the final verdict acquitting Borden is read. We finally enter her mind as she replays the fateful massacre during the moment the law releases her. In a bravura sequence that pushes network television standards and practices almost beyond the breaking point, she strips naked and, as the song says, "took an ax," butchering her brood amidst a burst of rapid-fire imagery; in slow motion, the yanked tube of blood, young Lizzie bounced on her father's knee, only a child's ghostly laughter on the soundtrack like raindrops in a country morning. And after being assaulted by a sensory deluge signifying her guilt, Lizzie is freed, enraging the aggressive and misogynistic prosecuting attorney (Ed Flanders) and greatly pleasing the nascent feminist community campaigning for her release.

The film ends on a note of ambiguity back at the house after Lizzie's sister asks her if she in fact committed the crimes and the camera makes a 360 track around the notorious woman as she stands silently, never answering. It is an appropriately tense and open conclusion, visually externalizing the story's quiet, simmering opacity, the restless spiral of Wendkos's camera conveying the unsettled character of Borden, who, despite her guilt, lives in a society that itself—in its treatment of women and children, and its reliance on overheated spectacle and rhetoric—is far from spotless. Wendkos made movies about unmoored lives, whether Sorel and Barbara's, Paula's, Lizzie Borden's or the dozens of other characters under his purview.

Other horror movies bearing his name are just as daring and unsettling as the aforementioned, from the 1972 *Haunts of the Very Rich* (mysterious, even avant-garde) to the expansive supernatural story *From the Dead of Night* (1989) to a superior adaptation of *The Bad Seed* from 1985. And even that lineup doesn't begin to encompass the miniseries, historical recreations, and crime sagas that strengthen the oeuvre like ballast. It is daunting, yes, but the work of Paul Wendkos in the horror genre is a great place to start exploring the work of this monumental director.

An All-Consuming Thing: An Interview with Curtis M. Lawson

David Peak

Curtis M. Lawson is my favorite type of writer. He is someone who quietly pursues deeply personal themes and obsessions in his writing, pushing the weird and horror into unique, frequently terrifying territory. In addition, he is active behind the scenes, producing episodes of his podcast, *Wyrd Transmissions,* and working with publisher Weird House Press alongside luminaries such as S. T. Joshi and Joe Morey to produce new and limited editions of important genre works.

Lawson's third collection, *The Envious Nothing: A Collection of Literary Ruin,* was released by Hippocampus Press in June 2022. Comprising both stories and poems, *The Envious Nothing* covers everything from the black vacuum of outer space to the folkloric aspects of haunted houses to apocalyptic theme parks, with several new stories appearing alongside those originally published in top-tier publications, such as *Doorbells at Dusk, In Darkness Delight,* and *Cosmic Horror Monthly.*

The following interview was conducted over email from July to November 2022.

David Peak: In the first story of your collection, "You and I and the Envious Nothing," the nothing is whatever remains in the void left by the Earth's destruction, something that is "envious of our will and imagination" that wants the last survivors of the human race to "be its conduit from nothing to something." What does adding "the" before "nothing" mean to you? And how does your conception of "the nothing" drive the horror in your stories?

Curtis M. Lawson: That's an interesting question. The self-deprecating part of myself wants to say I just thought it sounded cool and grandiose. Unconsciously, I probably ripped off the concept from *The Neverending Story,* and I'm sure that film had an impact on these stories. In that movie, the black wolf Gmork gives a speech about The Nothing that left a strong impression on me as a child. That said, I don't think I realized how much of an impact it had on these stories until the collection was complete.

On a more conscious level, I think that referring to *The Nothing* as such gives a force outside of existence a sense of personification. It asks the reader to think about the concept of Nothing with a capital N. What lies beyond creation? What existed before time? And what awaits our consciousness when our bodies fail and our synapses stop firing?

The Nothing drives each of the stories in different ways. In "You and I and the Envious Nothing" and "The Happiest Place on Earth," it is an all-devouring, antagonistic force. In "Secrets of the Forbidden Kata" and "Elvis and Isolde," it is a dangerous source of power that can be tapped. And in "She Born of Naught," it is a creative force that takes as it gives. I enjoyed looking at this concept from different angles and examining how exposure to this force beyond our concept of existence would impact different characters, as well as how it might manifest itself in various situations. It also lends itself to all sorts of thematic and subtextual motifs, which allowed me to examine deeper concepts.

DP: Let's talk about another concept that appears throughout your collection: Norse mythology. In particular, I was struck by your repeated references to Angrboða, the so-called "mother of monsters." Not only is she the subject of the poem that opens the book, but she is also mentioned in "Orphan," "Beneath the Emerald Sky," and "A Grave at the End of the World." In this last story, I loved how Angrboða was juxtaposed with modern technology, the Norns, in this instance a network of artificial intelligence. Can you talk a bit about the presence of Angrboða, or the wider influence of Norse mythology, on your writing?

CML: I've always had a deep fascination with Norse mythology. It started when I was quite young, and I fell deeper into it through a fascination with fantasy and gaming and then paganism and occultism in my early teens. My involvement with the black metal subculture a few years later would urge me deeper down the rabbit hole.

Toying with the themes of Norse mythology in art is nothing new for me. When I used to play in bands, I wrote a lot of songs with strong Nordic imagery. Fittingly, Nordic esoteric ideas have worked their way into many of my stories, and references to aspects of different Asatru subcultures have appeared in my work. In fact, my first novel, *The Devoured,* examined cosmic horror through the lenses of Norse and Native American myth.

Historically, my main interest has been in understanding the symbolism behind the character of Odin. I've always been drawn to the concepts of self-sacrifice and persona. In recent years, I've been fascinated by the figure of Angrboða, the wife of Loki and the mother of Hel, Fenris, and Jörmungandr. I haven't come across too much information about her in the original myths, or in the books I've read—just snippets that reveal a deeply enigmatic figure. I'm interested in reading more about the left-hand path tradition of Thursatru and seeing if there is a deeper examination of Angrboða in those texts.

Even though she isn't front and center during Ragnarök or as ostentatiously evil as Surt, Loki, or her monstrous children, in many ways she heralded the end and set the stage for the twilight of the gods. Because of that, she seemed like a perfect figure to serve as the herald of The Nothing for my book.

Beyond Angrboða, Norse myth is prevalent throughout the collection, and my body of work as a whole. There are hints to another Nordic figure in "Elvis and Isolde," but I don't explicitly state it there, so I feel I should leave it to the reader to notice it or not. Rune magic is also referenced in several stories in *The Envious Nothing,* and I find it satisfying to examine myths at deeper than a surface level. I like to incorporate some of the subtext, and even the personal meaning I find in them, into my own narratives.

DP: You mentioned your involvement in black metal. One of my favorite stories in your collection is "Orphan," which is about a punk rock musician named Ian Abyss whose misanthropic lyrics and worldview ultimately reveal his place in a very special family. You also wrote the novel *Black Heart Boys' Choir,* which is about a teenage musical prodigy. How has music influenced your writing?

CML: Music was the first way I actively tried to express myself, and I was a musician for a long time before I started writing in earnest. As a music lover, especially someone so entrenched in a particular subculture, it came to color how I view most things. In my adolescence, my musical taste dictated who I was friends with, the girls I was attracted to, how I dressed, the spirituality I explored, and the books I read. It was an all-consuming thing for me.

Still, almost two decades since I quit my last band, I view a lot of life in musical terms. I see repeating patterns in my life or in my writing as leitmotifs. I consider the rhythms of my days and of my words. I use terms such as *dissonance* and *resolution* when talking about periods of chaos or order that I've gone through. Music informs how I see and make sense of the world.

Aside from having a slightly musical approach to how I use language, music has informed my writing in other ways. *Black Heart Boys' Choir* is structured like a piece of music, or at least that was my intention. I repeat several sentences and even entire paragraphs throughout the book, almost like a refrain. The book is also broken up into movements—and one of them is a waltz. The chapters in that section are arranged as triplets to mimic 3/4 timing. Theme one, theme two, theme three, repeat. One, two, three. One, two, three.

One of the things I wanted to touch upon in "Orphan" was the importance that music plays in the lives of certain individuals, particularly at-risk youth. When I was growing up, there was this stigma about punk rock, metal, and hip hop that led to negative lifestyles and poor choices. There was some truth to that, but no more than the beer-commercial culture that TV sold all of us. What really scared adults at the time was that these types of music offered glimpses into other alternative approaches to life.

There was this bohemian aspect to those genres, but they

also shined light on movements such as straight edge, neo-paganism, and anarchism. These movements—and underground music in general—have helped so many kids survive traumatic childhoods and realize that there is more to the world than their dysfunctional homes and the mindless bullies they go to school with. A sense of belonging can give someone a place to feel at home when the rest of the world has rejected them. I don't think it's an exaggeration to say that without finding a home in music as a kid, I probably would have ended up doing something violent and stupid. I'm sure I'm not the only one.

DP: On that point, I've always seen writing weird fiction, or horror or whatever you want to call it, as a way or rejecting the monoculture. At its best, weird fiction expresses how we experience reality in individual ways. It's sort of like how exposure to The Nothing can change our concept of existence, as you said. On this point, one of your recent tweets asked about the concept of subcultural appropriation, and that got me thinking about authenticity in fiction, particularly weird fiction, which often concerns itself with irreality. For instance, Richard Gavin, who frequently writes about the occult, is a practicing occultist. Christopher Slatsky's stories contain so much research that some readers mistake them for nonfiction. It's clear to me that many of the topics that inform your writing—mysticism, the occult, musicality—are deeply personal. Do you think this is a core component of weird fiction?

CML: I do think that is a core part of making successful weird fiction, or I should say, it's integral to creating the kind of story I see as successful. Weird fiction, probably all fiction, is best when it comes from a place of emotional and intellectual honesty from the author.

Clive Barker's visceral, sexually driven writing works because these are things that move him, so they're part of the DNA of many of his stories. His imitators lack that genuine, intimate obsession with the carnal, so their stories don't hold the same weight. People lift tentacles and cursed books from Lovecraft, but what made Lovecraft's work great was the conviction of his fears and shortcomings and how they shined through. Ligotti's pessimism is palpable and legitimate, so his work is powerful in turn.

In regards to my proposal of subcultural appropriation, I think people should be able to dress how they want, borrow aspects of whatever art or aesthetic makes them happy, but for me, there is something cheap about imitating the superficial aspects of someone else's art or lifestyle or whatever. It's so much more rewarding to speak your own truth, and it shows in the quality of art that one produces.

DP: What are some examples of recent horror fiction that you think is particularly successful? And why? What are you looking for when you pick up a new book or start reading a short story?

CML: There are so many great works coming out recently. Maybe it's recency bias, or just that this is "my time," but I feel like we are living through this renaissance of horror and the weird. Sure, the market is a bit saturated, and there is a lot that isn't so great, but people are going in so many interesting directions, not just from being underrepresented and having a chance to tell their stories, but in ways that are evolving horror narratives, taking bold chances with storytelling, and exploring old tropes in new ways.

What I'm looking for in fiction first and foremost is to be entertained. But the books and stories that really stick with me are the ones that get me thinking. They might leave me pondering some deep existential problem or unanswered questions in the narrative, expose insecurities in myself or my beliefs, or make me rethink how story and structure can work. I like thought-provoking fiction best of all. The caveat is that I hate being told what to think. I have little patience for heavy-handedness in fiction, and I want an artist to present me with questions to think about, rather than their answers.

B. R. Yeager's *Negative Space* immediately comes to mind. There is this wonderful ambiguity to the story that is centered on a character whom we only ever get to see through the perceptions of others. It raises so many more questions than it answers and it lingers in your brain after you read it.

Elana Gomel recently published a phenomenal collection of gothic fairytales called *My Lady of Plagues*. She really understands the nature of fairytales and approaches them in a very dark and old-school way, but her writing is accessible for the modern reader. She also wrote a novella called *Little Sister* that takes place in a kind of nightmarish, wonderland version of the Soviet Union.

Another one I love is *Corpsepaint,* and I'm not just saying that because you're interviewing me. We've already talked about my history with black metal—and that book was just perfect for me. You explored the cursed or haunted music trope in a very modern and dirty way, and you really nailed a lot of the subtleties of black metal that might be missed by someone who merely has a passing interest in the genre. If you look at a book like Joe Hill's *Heart-Shaped Box,* it's a fine ghost story, but the subcultural elements seem very disingenuous. You can tell it was written by someone looking from the outside in.

Arrangements in Adamantine

The joey Zone

SAX ROHMER. *The Whispering Mummy and Others*. Edited by S. T. Joshi. New York: Hippocampus Press, 2023. 295 pp. $20.00 tpb. ISBN: 9781614983798.

> You know how dusk falls in Egypt? At one moment the sky is a brilliant canvas, glorious with every color known to art, at the next the curtain—the wonderful veil of deepest violet–has fallen: the stars break through it like diamonds through the finest gauze . . .

It has been a decade since these words were in legitimate print and they still shine like diamonds.

In 2013 Centipede Press published *Brood of the Witch-Queen,* a collection of fifteen short stories and Rohmer's novel *Brood of the Witch-Queen*. This collection, the twelfth title in Hippocampus Press' Classics of Gothic Horror series, features the same stories as that volume, omitting only the titular novel. The cover by Aeron Alfrey is a three-dimensional fever dream bearing a slight resemblance to W. T. Benda's iconic design of *The Mask of Fu Manchu* (1932).

Sax Rohmer (pseudonym of Arthur Sarsfield Ward, 1883–1959) has resided for decades on this reviewer's shelf alongside such writers as M. P. Shiel, Sapper, and Dennis Wheatley. Famous as the chronicler of That Most Honorable Eastern Physician, Rohmer neither originated the "Yellow Peril" trope (perhaps Shiel) nor overextended stereotypes beyond their cultural shelf life (as much as Wheatley). Moriarty is more than matched by Holmes, but Nayland Smith is a mere cipher compared to the charismatic doctor. As with Edgar Rice Burroughs's Tarzan books, however, this series is only a small part of the author's total output.

Of the supernaturally infused novels S. T. Joshi mentions in his introduction, we should add *Grey Face* (1924) as worthy of revival, definitely using its original jacket depicting the title anti-hero's hypnotic visage. What we have in this present volume are stories culled from *Tales of Secret Egypt* (1918), *The Haunting of Low Fennel* (1920), and *Tales of Chinatown* (1922). Sax is, geographically, all over the place, whether in London, Limehouse, the English countryside, or Burma. But his main port of call is Cairo. Saville Granger in the story "The Curse of a Thousand Kisses" is really just a stand-in for Rohmer. And the rest of us:

> I had for many years cherished a secret ambition to pay a protracted visit to Egypt, but the ties of an arduous profession hitherto had rendered its realisation impossible. Now, a stranger in a strange land, I found myself *at home* . . . the only real happiness I ever knew—indeed, as I soon began to realise, had ever known—I found among the discordant cries and mingled smells of perfume and decay in the native city . . . it was the people, the shops, the shuttered houses, the noises and smells of the Eastern streets which gripped my heart.

Tales of Secret Egypt highlights the hubris of The Occidental, which merits a role in comedy, more ofttimes, tragedy. Neither hero or villain, the self-appointed majordomo of this locale is one Abû Tabâh, "black robed, white turbaned, and urbane, his delicate ivory hands resting upon the head of an ebony came . . . a veritable presence . . . his eyes . . . like the eyes of a gazelle." "The Whispering Mummy" has Tabâh and a negligible narrator help uncover the sleight-of-hand that is neither benevolent nor the sweet nothings murmured by a desert lich. Two outright weird tales, "In the Valley of the Sorceress" and "Lord of the Jackals," result in comedy and tragedy respectively, the first favoring Bast while the second engenders sympathy—certainly not for the main "protagonist" but the Lord of its title—Hayil Anubis!

Of the three Rohmer collections from which this material has been sourced, of most interest to readers is *The Haunting of Low Fennel*. Besides the aforementioned "Curse of a Thousand Kisses" (with its namedrop of William Beckford's classic *Vathek* [1786]), we have an eerie drama set in Burma, "The Valley of the Just," and "The Master of Hollow Grange." There is a great buildup of suspense in the latter, only to have the author feint with the weak hand-off: "That there were horrors—monstrosities that may not be described, whose names may not be written"! Although Joshi says "it's super-naturalism is unconvincingly accounted for," this writer thinks the title story "The Haunting of Low Fennel" is a prime example of the writer at his most entertaining.

The employment of the stereotype of a blustering ex-military man is a characterization used in several Rohmer tales, in this case in the person of one Major Dale: "If Low Fennel is not haunted, I'm a Dutchman, by the Lord Harry!" Such comic interjections in these stories leaven the literal miasma of fear, as opposed to just annoying by juxtaposition. This miasma:

> had the form of a man, but the face [was] not of a man, but a ghoul! . . .
>
> . . . The chin and lower lip of this awful face seemed to be drawn up so as almost to meet the nose, entirely covering the upper lip and the nostrils were distended to an incredible degree, whilst the skin had a sort of purple tinge . . .

The dust jacket of the Pearson first edition of *Low Fennel* features this afrit, albeit with less Pickmanesque physiognomy. The narrator deduces that the haunting is

> something older than the house, older perhaps, than the very hills . . . something as old as the root of all evil, and it dwells in the Ancient British tumulus . . .
>
> . . . Barrows and tumuli of the stone and bronze age, and also Roman shrines, seem frequently to be productive of such emanations.

Major Dale will have none of this folk horror:

> Then is the place haunted by the spirit of some uneasy Ancient Briton or something of that sort, Addison? Hang it all! You can't tell me a fairy tale like that! A ghost going back to pre-Roman days is a bit too ancient for me, my boy—too hoary, by the Lord Harry!

Tales of Chinatown's 1949 Popular Library edition boasts a superb Rudolph Belarski cover depicting "The Hand of the Mandarin Quong." This book also contains Rohmer's finest short story, "Tchériapin," with its fatalistic narrative of revenge employing "magic" somewhat prefiguring that in A. Merritt's *Burn, Witch, Burn!* (1933). Reprinted many times— Virgil Finlay's illustration for its appearance in *Famous Fantastic Mysteries* of July 1951 being notable—the plot of this tale need not be elaborated upon; suffice it to say the dark beauty of its telling has a denouement as "hard as a diamond." If there is one reason to add this Hippocampus collection of Sax Rohmer to your bookshelf, this and accompanying arrangements in adamantine are requisite to full celebration of the Black Mass that is classic horror.

The Literary Adolescence of a Grandmaster

Darrell Schweitzer

RAY BRADBURY. *The Earliest Bradbury*. Edited and written by David Ritter and Daniel Ritter. N.p.: First Fandom Experience, 2020. 164 pp. $125.00 hc. Second edition. ISBN: 9781733296489.

Has this book really been out for more than two years? It is not clear to me if this "second edition" is brand new, or what changes were made between it and the first edition. A new "edition" usually implies some changes, as opposed to merely a new printing.

But never mind that. I confess I had never heard of it, or First Fandom Experience, until I encountered their table at the Boskone convention in Boston this past February. Of course, I knew what First Fandom was. It was an organization of "the Dinosaurs of Science Fiction," and while they may have bent the rules a bit toward the end, the basic membership requirement was that you had to show some activity in science fiction fandom prior to 1939, which was the *annus mirabilis* in which the Golden Age of Science Fiction officially began with the July *Astounding* (the first issue in which John W. Campbell, Jr. had full control) and the first World Science Fiction Convention was held in New York. Attendance at that Worldcon would clinch it, but a letter published in a prozine or a fanzine prior to that point would also do.

Alas, with the recent passing of Robert A. Madle at age 102, there simply are no First Fandomites left. First Fandom Experience is apparently a successor organization devoted to publishing incredibly deluxe coffee-table books showcasing to the early days of the fannish subculture. What most attracted my attention at that Boskone table was the display copy of *The Visual History of Science Fiction Fandom: The 1930s,* which is priced on the organization's website at $195.00 a copy.

That may seem steep, but as I paged through it, marveling at the unending stream of photos and facsimile reproductions of ancient fanzine pages (many of them hectographed, in faint blue type, which was somehow rendered legible), it was explained to me by the gentleman at the table that these books cost something like $125.00 a copy to print. By the logic of normal book publishing, where the list price should be four to five times the cost of production, that would make for a $500 book, which nobody could afford. So First Fandom Experience is barely making back costs.

First Fandom Experience books are large, glossy, all-color volumes that convey the early science fiction fan world through reproductions of fabulously rare documents. Those hectographed fanzines can fade if exposed to light for a few hours, and print runs were seldom as high as a hundred. Only a very few have survived, mostly in the collections of the last First Fans, so we're looking at the equivalent of lost scraps from the Library of Alexandria.

When I was handed a copy of their Bradbury book with the request that I review it somewhere, I was under a moral obligation to do so. Freeloading on such an epic scale cannot go unrequited.

If you are a Bradbury fan, you need this book. You might be able to get it for less than $125 if you can find it at a convention, so that the FFE people don't have to ship it priority mail. The price at Boskone itself was $75.00.

The Earliest Ray Bradbury is, unsurprisingly, a stunning production. Virtually every page has a color reproduction of something, if only typewritten text on browning fanzine paper. It is a collection of the earliest surviving Bradbury writings, from the years 1937 to 1941, cutting off right as Bradbury sold his first professional stories to the pulps. As most of these are very short items, interspersed with commentary by the Ritters, the effect is more that of a scrapbook and a biography. Here is as clear a picture as we will ever get of the early Bradbury, a teenager just out of high school (college was not an option for him in the Great Depression) who sold newspapers on street corners and attended meetings of the Los Angeles Science Fiction Society on roller-skates because he did not have money for the trolley. He was by all indications loud, bumptious, and determined to be a funnyman. Virtually all his earliest writings are attempts at humor. Maybe his jokes lose something without him telling them, but they seem pretty lame on the page.

I confess I once blackmailed Bradbury with one of these. Well, I exaggerate, but so did he when he was writing this stuff. About 1970 a friend gave me a photocopy of "I am Positively Not Robert Bloch!" (included here), which I proposed to reprint as a curiosity in my own fanzine, *Procrastination*. It is certainly curious, if not very good. Bradbury looks in the mirror and interviews himself. He sees:

> . . . my reflection gnashed its teeth and made as if to bite me. Gad. What a face! That yellow hair tousling down in rumpled reams, those scarlet lips like pomegranate seeds thanx to Seabury Quinn. That slavering row of bicuspids, interspersed with pop-corn and chewing gum.

Like all Bradbury fanzine writings, this was uncopyrighted and I could have just reprinted it, but one of the reasons I survived my own adolescence is that I wasn't stupid enough to screw with the likes of Ray Bradbury. I politely wrote to him and asked permission. He replied, in effect, "No, please don't! Take this instead!" He sent me his essay "My New Ending to *Rosemary's Baby*," which had recently appeared in the *Los Angeles Times*. I duly printed it. Years later Bradbury's bibliographer, Donn Albright, called me up to confirm that this printing, one of the rarest of all Bradbury items, actually existed.

In his lifetime Bradbury did his best to keep his early fanzine effusions out of professional print. It is easy to understand why, and, as a writer myself with roots in fanzine fandom, I am glad that I will never be famous enough for such a book of my infantile scribblings to be of any interest. But Bradbury's *are* of interest, and presented in this context, as a scrapbook/biography, their republication is welcome and valuable.

To be candid, if I have been shown Bradbury's literary output circa 1939, I would not have been aware that he showed any particular promise beyond his eagerness and energy. When he met Julius Schwartz at the Worldcon in New York in 1939, Bradbury asked him to be his agent, and Schwartz said, "Keep trying, kid." (Later Schwartz did become his agent, very successfully.) In retrospect we may be able to spot a flash of talent here and there, some touching on a theme Bradbury later developed successfully, but he clearly had a long way to go.

The important lesson here, which you need to keep in mind if you're teaching writing or running a workshop, is that nobody, however unpromising, is hopeless unless they show no improvement over a long period of time, perhaps ten years. But five years after Bradbury's first story "Hollerbochen's Dilemma" appeared in *Imagination!* in 1938, he was publishing "R Is for Rocket" (a.k.a. "The King of the Gray Spaces") in *Famous Fantastic Mysteries* and such wonderful stories as "The Wind" and "The Scythe" in *Weird Tales*. Twelve years later he was the author of *The Martian Chronicles*. The transformation had been miraculous. What we have in *The Earliest Bradbury* is a record of the author's creative life right up to the point where the miracle happened.

We can see that on his road to greatness, Bradbury had to shed certain influences. The first of these was Forrest J Ackerman. Ackerman may have been the young Bradbury's mentor and lifelong friend, but he was also given to juvenile, wiseass writing filled with puns, slang, portmanteau words, and borderline gibberish. ("Hollerbochen lookt into the future with his magic mind. He wisht he nevr'd found the fateful power he possesst so strongly.") Ackerman may have developed an amusing (or annoying) personal style along these lines in the pages of *Famous Monsters of Filmland* years later, but Ackermanese was not right for Ray Bradbury.

He had to understand that he wasn't a funnyman. His pal Robert Bloch could be funny and sell the result, but Bradbury could not. That was because Bloch was writing complete stories, not short squibs.

Bradbury's early friendship with Robert A. Heinlein (whom he knew through LASFS) was very helpful. Heinlein convinced him that real stories are about real people and real emotions, not just clever twists on neat ideas. As any short fiction editor knows, to this day, this delusion persists among slushpile writers. A neat idea—which is probably not as clever or as neat as you think it is—is not the same thing as a story. Bradbury had to learn to write stories.

He also needed to expose himself to a wider range of literature. He had to look beyond the contents of *Thrilling Wonder* or even *Astounding* of the late '30s if he was to get anywhere. It was probably very helpful that he spent much of his four-day bus ride back to California from the 1939 Worldcon reading *The Grapes of Wrath*.

There was one fanzine story (included here) that showed some promise. "Luana the Living" appeared in *Polaris* in 1940. It is a few thousand words long, and is not gimmicky science fiction, but a horror story of the sort Bradbury would soon be writing for *Weird Tales*. It begins:

> Before I conclude this mundane existence, bid the terrors of the alien farewell, and take my leave of things light and dark, I must tell someone the reason for my suicide. A horror clings malignantly to my brain, and far back in the recesses of the subconscious it burns like the pale flame of a candle in the tombs of the dead. It steals my strength and leaves me weak and trembling like a child. Try as I will, I cannot rid myself of it, for the night of the full Moon forces its return.

No, this isn't about a werewolf. It's about a man who ventured into unknown jungle regions of India (about which Bradbury apparently knew nothing, save that there are tigers there), and after several hundred words about how hot, spooky, and generally unpleasant the jungle is, he comes upon savage "natives" engaged in some kind of hideous rite beneath the full moon. Eventually some of this becomes intelligible "in the tongue of the ancient Hindus" and takes on a decidedly anti-colonialist tenor ("Living Luana! . . . Keep from us from the unholy spirit of the white man!"), whereupon our hero intervenes and shoots several of the natives. The rest scatter, but one of them, dying, pronounces an eternal curse on the blasphemer (and murderer) and he is indeed cursed, haunted by the moon or moon goddess wherever he goes, driven to despair and death. This is a routine, badly overwritten "native curse" story, but Bradbury aficionados will appreciate how he developed exactly the same plot structure into the much more successful "The Wind" about two years later.

What we notice here, too, is that the opening paragraph reads an awful lot like Lovecraft, or bad imitation Lovecraft. Fortunately, this was one more influence that Bradbury rapidly shed. Lovecraft's voice was not Bradbury's. It would not have made him unique.

The real strength Bradbury had, early on, other than his boundless energy, was a willingness to learn, from Heinlein, and particularly from Leigh Brackett, who met him every week at Venice Beach and critiqued his latest stories. She was only five years older than Bradbury and had just sold her first stories in 1940, but she knew a lot he needed to learn and she was able to teach him. In one sense, *The Earliest Bradbury* very clearly shows us the author's path to grandmastership. Step by step, he had to learn *not* to write like most of the examples that are gathered here.

If that seems like a backhanded compliment, it shouldn't be taken as one. *The Earliest Bradbury* is superbly presented, very entertaining, and for the fannish historian, Bradbury biographer, or would-be writer, quite educational.

Deterritorializing a Genre
toward the Infinite

Géza A. G. Reilly

MICHAEL CISCO. *Weird Fiction: A Genre Study*. London: Palgrave Macmillan, 2022. 340 pp. $119.99 hc. ISBN: 9783030924492. $89.00 ebook. ISBN: 9783030924508.

"Genre" is one of those things that most people think they have a handle on. The genre of a piece of fiction is what category the fiction can be slotted into based on the qualities present in that fiction, right? Like, we know it's a Western because it has cowboys in it. There's even a horse. Sure, there might be issues in there—like, for example, the way in which the movie *Cowboys and Aliens* could easily be classified as a Western *or* a Science Fiction story and therefore could be found in either category's section on a streaming service without fitting comfortably into either. Still, the *standard* holds and is of utility even if there are outliers.

However, genre is more complicated than that. The above method of placing a given work of fiction within a particular genre category based upon the tropes (or other features) within that work results in genre being little more than a classificatory tool. It's useful for sorting works, in other words, but it does next to nothing in terms of providing insight into any specific piece of fiction other than charting its surface features. A much more nuanced and less transcendental understanding of genre allows us to realize that "genres," per se, do not exist. Or, rather, they do exist, but only insofar as we understand a set of complex relationships between authorial intention, words on the page, and audience expectation. In other words, if we think of genre as an *analytic tool* rather than a process of systematized classification, we can use genre to gain insight into specific works rather than simply determine what goes where on our shelves.

Michael Cisco's *Weird Fiction: A Genre Study* is a fine example of both how rewarding and how difficult a robust understanding of genre can be. Drawing primarily on his deep understanding of theorists Gilles Deleuze and Félix Guattari, Cisco spends his time in this dense book laying out the foundations of his understanding of the genre of weird fiction across four initial chapters followed by a series of case studies that demonstrate the utility of his formulation. Cisco rejects or dialectically absorbs prior genre studies (Todorov, Kristeva, Carroll, etc.) to develop a theoretical understanding of weird fiction as a genre that is ultimately simple in summary yet substantive in full development.

In brief, Cisco argues for the existence of three basic elements that arise from weird fictions and allow us greater analytic understanding of those texts: "a bizarre encounter, which is the self-difference of the ordinary, that marks a character with a destiny, which is change, in order to produce the supernatural, understood here to mean a sense of the infinity of experience involving the limits of reality, for the reader." What this focus on the bizarre, a destiny, and the supernatural does is allow weird fiction to remain grounded in *this* world, the prosaic world we all know and navigate, *but* forces us to confront the fact that experience and our identities are fundamentally unbounded in ways we cannot predict. This focus on the world as it is both echoes Lovecraft's insistence on weird fiction possessing a singular break from material reality and allows Cisco to differentiate weird fiction from other genres. Fantasy, for example, deals with similar "breaks" in observable existence. However, it is the fact that the supernatural in fantasy necessitates jumping the tracks, as it were, from one world into another (Narnia, Middle Earth, Hyperborea, etc.) that means that fantasy cannot itself be weird fiction. The weird, it seems, is a condition of *this* world.

Cisco also argues that artistic works can be separated into "major" and "minor" camps (an idea borrowed from Deleuze and Guattari) and plays with the idea to determine what there is "to weird fiction apart from recycling a handful of clichés." Major works can be thought of as commercial or imitative texts (the aforementioned clichés), while minor works can be thought of as innovative or groundbreaking. It should be noted that the distinction between major and minor works is not necessarily a value judgment; both sets of texts can be analyzed to powerful results. As Cisco frames it, the distinction between the two is that fictions in the major mode ultimately "develop into a judgment against those who do not maintain and desire the standards of the everyday," while fictions in the minor mode "[issue] a warning: do not cling to identity, all experience is infinite, and so you will no longer be who you now are." The former results in a deterritorialization of existence followed by an immediate settling of the ground beneath us, while the latter keeps that deterritorialization open, allowing the possibility of infinite continual discovery. While both allow for the fundamental change of those involved (including, interestingly, the reader), the major mode locks down the weird and makes it known while the minor mode uses the weird as a signpost pointing toward ever greater instability.

It is important to reiterate that Cisco's schema is an analytic tool rather than a classificatory one, and this is laid bare in the almost two-thirds of the book that is spent on Cisco's case studies of twenty-nine stories. By presenting us with summaries of each story's bizarre encounter, mark of destiny, and supernatural result followed by analysis of the story on those terms and in terms of its major and minor elements, Cisco demonstrates that his study is not interested in creating a means of separating one work from another for the purposes of establishing a transcendent standard against which other works could be held. Rather, *Weird Fiction* presents us with a method that could be used to analyze any given work without needing to worry about what conceptual box that work fits into. Even the two approaches discussed above are not a standard to be applied *to* narratives so much as they are what could arise *out* of a dedicated and careful reading of works— allowing us to think of them as weird fiction based on what we discover within them.

Would there be benefit in doing so? Analytically, I suspect so. Although I think there might be quibble room in Cisco's theoretical approach (there almost always is, since this is theory and praxis demands we refine our methods as we implement them), I must admit that he has provided an understanding of weird fiction that far outstrips even the most entrenched approaches to genre theory. Even the best-known genre studies of weird fiction, such as *The Weird Tale* by S. T. Joshi and *Supernatural Horror in Literature* by H. P. Lovecraft, do not present anywhere near the level of rigor that Cisco brings to bear on his subject. This is not to say that those studies are not worth reading, of course, but after finishing *Weird Fiction* I find it difficult to think of them as more than the fertile soil that Cisco was able to grow out of.

Genre theory is not what we traditionally expect. It is far more than a mere classificatory tool, and in fact a robust understanding of genre theory can help us understand why texts were produced, why they were read, why they *continue* to be produced, and why they *continue* to be read. Scholars and critics have been developing genre theory for decades, and for each step forward there is seemingly always lacunae—what about *this* text, *this* genre, *this* author, or *this* audience? Michael Cisco has addressed one of those lacunae, and he has done so persuasively. Indeed, one could even suggest that Cisco's book deterritorializes the ground of weird fiction as a whole and, as a result, opens our eyes to the infinite possibilities within that genre—and, thereby, in existence. Although *Weird Fiction* would probably be more enjoyable to those of a particular academic bent, much the same could be said about its subject matter. Ultimately, Cisco has provided us with a real achievement, and those who wish to come to a deeper understanding of the genre they enjoy—and push that understanding outwards into heretofore unknown conclusions—would benefit well from grappling with it.

Audible Nightmares: Thomas Ligotti's Penguin Classic Becomes an Audiobook

Oliver Sheppard

THOMAS LIGOTTI. *Songs of a Dead Dreamer and Grimscribe*. Foreword by Jeff VanderMeer. Narrated by Jon Padgett and Linda Jones. New York: Penguin Audio. $30. 1315 mins. ISBN: 9780593682913.

In a 2014 article for Vulture.com, horror writer Jeff Vander-Meer lamented that, at that time, Thomas Ligotti did not have "a mainstream literary publisher [to] give him the push needed to reach a wider audience." So VanderMeer issued a plea: "Library of America, are you listening? Think of [Ligotti] as the Steven Millhauser of the weird and just jump right in there, headfirst."

Within a year of this appeal, Penguin Random House (and not, it should be noted, Library of America) answered the call, announcing the publication of a book-length collection of Thomas Ligotti's weird horror fiction. They even enlisted VanderMeer to write the foreword. *Songs of a Dead Dreamer and Grimscribe* was to be a single book comprised of two previous collections of Thomas Ligotti's short stories. The move was welcomed by Ligotti fans who felt HBO's *True Detective* had already lifted many of his ideas for that show's first season's mainstream success. Published in October 2015, Penguin's 448-page omnibus debuted under the prestigious "Penguin Classics" banner. And this put Thomas Ligotti—who up until then had mainly been a niche/cult horror author—into the select company of such living literary giants as Thomas Pynchon and Don DeLillo. (Let's put aside for the moment that Morrissey—yes, *that* Morrissey—can also be counted among the ten living authors honored with a Penguin Classics publishing credit. *Oof.*)

Fast-forward eight years to March 2023, and we finally have the arrival of the official audiobook of Thomas Ligotti's *Songs of a Dead Dreamer and Grimscribe* from Penguin Audio. The 2015 Penguin Classics debut was a coup for those who had long advocated for the importance of the reclusive horror author, and not least among these advocates—nay, among the front ranks, even, of Ligotti's *evangelists*—has been Jon Padgett, a horror author of no mean talent himself. (Padgett needs no introduction to the readers of these pages.) It is only fitting that Padgett should be the primary narrator of the *Songs of a Dead Dreamer and Grimscribe* audiobook, the definitive audio version of the definitive collection for which he helped pave the way. Joining him in reading is co-narrator Linda Jones, herself an experienced voice acting talent; her horror credits include impressive narrations of Shirley Jackson's darkest material, much of it also issued by Penguin Random House.

The new audiobook of *Songs of a Dead Dreamer and Grimscribe* consists of about 22 hours' worth of narrated material. This is about double the size of a typical audiobook. (And if this were a band, that would be approximately 26 full-length LPs!) But, lest that nearly 22 hours of listening time sound daunting, it is worth keeping in mind that the whole of this audiobook *is comprised of more than 30 short stories*. (The number of stories in *Songs of a Dead Dreamer and Grimscribe* can vary depending on how one counts them. For example, Ligotti's "Nyctalops Trilogy" is in this collection, and one could count that as one whole story or as three separate tales, depending on taste.) In any event, the almost 22 hours of audio material here are divided between 30 to 34 short stories, averaging out to an eminently reasonable half an hour (or so) per tale. The audiobook is divided into easily digestible chunks, in other words, well suited for listening while on a lunch break, while walking, before bed, etc. Indeed, listening to many of these stories while going on a sunset walk might be the perfect way to enjoy these dark gems of modern Gothic prose.

At this point in time, Jon Padgett is no stranger to providing spoken-word readings of Ligotti's work on recorded format: Cadabra Records, for example, has, at the time of this writing, released at least five 12-inch vinyl records of Padgett's readings of various of Ligotti's short fiction, one short story per offering. It is worth noting here that the Cadabra recording imprint was founded by hardcore guitarist and artist Jonathan Dennison, who owns, as well, Chiroptera Press, which has recently published Ligotti's long-awaited *Pictures of Apocalypse* poetry collection. This collection came out around the same time Penguin Random House released its *Songs of a Dead Dreamer and Grimscribe* audiobook under review here. (Indeed, March 2023 has been a banner month for many things Ligotti!)

Readers of *Dead Reckonings* almost certainly know what to expect with the content of the audiobook version *of Songs of a Dead Dreamer and Grimscribe*. After its debut in 2015, the Penguin collection quickly became the main entry point into all things Ligotti. And for the public at large it still serves as the most easily accessible on-ramp to which advocates can point when others wonder where to start with Ligotti's sometimes perplexingly disparate (if not downright hard-to-find) corpus of work. The world of 2023 is such that many consumers nowadays prefer podcasts and audio material to printed text; and so this audio edition of the Penguin Classics collection is sure to be the main introductory work for most new Thomas Ligotti fans.

"[O]ther realms are always capable of making their presence felt, hovering unseen like strange cities disguised as clouds or hidden like a world of pale specters within a fog," Ligotti writes in "In the Shadow of Another World," read here by Jon Padgett. "One is besieged by orders of entity that refuse to articulate their exact nature or proper milieu."

This paragraph sums up much of the eerie impact that one feels, almost as if from instinct, from Thomas Ligotti's writing. Padgett's soft vocal warble makes for pleasant listening that—as I mentioned before—would make this audiobook excellent listening fare on headphones during a sunset stroll, or around a campfire on a crisp October night. And given how much Padgett has done to ensure Ligotti's legacy as one of America's premiere writers of literary dark fiction, it is probably right that he should be narrating these stories himself—

yet, as friends of his endeavors, we should perhaps also gently remind him that he doesn't have to be all things Ligotti to all people at all times. By this I mean that while listening to this audiobook there are times when Padgett's friendly, sometimes even "camp guidance counselor" voice dulls some of the impact of the darker edges of Ligotti's most brutal prose moments.

Of course, Padgett has served as both the August Derleth and Donald Wandrei to Thomas Ligotti's H. P. Lovecraft, both by way of his decades-old *Thomas Ligotti Online* website and by virtue of his Grimscribe Press, which is a tribute to Ligotti in a similar sense that Derleth and Wandrei's Arkham House was a tribute to Lovecraft. Yet Ligotti is still alive; and while Padgett has started the official website, the press, and the journal *Vastarien*—which is the "Ligotti Studies" literary journal *par excellence*—it doesn't need to be the case that Padgett should also feel he must be the official and/or primary voice actor for all Ligotti's prose, too. (He has earned the right at this point to have that burden shouldered by someone else!) Audio-wise, Ligotti's darkest work would be served well by someone with a baritone or bass timbre in their delivery— someone who registers in their vocal delivery a hint of the sinister; perhaps an Alan Rickman–type vocal narrator, darkly Gothic and evincing a malevolent edge in their diction as needed. And yet, having said that, there are many unofficial readings of Ligotti's works already out there on places like YouTube and TikTok, and none of them are as good, ultimately, as the production afforded here by Jon Padgett and Linda Jones.

Nightmares Inspired by an Uncertain Future

Greg Gbur

Mooncalves: Strange Stories. Edited by John WM Thompson. Oregon: NO Press. 306 pp. $40.00 hc. ISBN: 9798985254501; $8.00 ebook.

Usually, when I read a new anthology of horror fiction, I have some idea of what to expect in terms of theme or subject matter. This was not the case when I began reading *Mooncalves,* a hefty collection of stories edited by John WM Thompson, which was released in ebook form in March 2023, with a limited edition hardcover appearing in April. This ignorance on my part ended up making the book a delightful surprise, as I never knew what to expect with each new turn of the page.

Mooncalves contains twenty-three stories of original fiction, all recent, by an impressive range of weird fiction authors. There are a number of names that will be immediately familiar to fans, such as Lisa Tuttle and Steve Rasnic Tem, as well as many that will probably be new to readers. All the stories are fascinating, unusual, and unsettling.

So what is *Mooncalves* about? We gain a clue from the title itself, which I am embarrassed to say is a word I was not familiar with. The term first originated in the sixteenth century and refers to a monstrous birth, either human or bovine, blamed on the powers of the moon. "Mooncalf" evolved to refer to any sort of monstrous or deformed being. In modern times, its meaning has softened to refer to a "foolish person" or a "person who spends their time daydreaming."

All these definitions apply to the stories of *Mooncalves*. The tales are surreal, often grotesque, and seemingly half-formed, leaving many unanswered questions for the reader to ponder. These descriptions are intended as compliments. The unknown is a powerful source of dread and uncertainty, and the tales in the anthology tap into it directly.

A few short descriptions will give an idea of the contents of the volume. In Briar Ripley Page's opening "December Story," a man receives a letter from a former lover and begins to worry about their fate, as the letter is frustratingly ambiguous. Their eventual reunion does not go as either of them expected. In Ernest O. Ògúnyẹmí's "The Tomato," a woman comes to believe that her son has been turned into a literal tomato, and her increasing desperation to save him leads her to dark places. (The premise sounds absurd, but the story is quite horrifying.)

In Adam Golaski's "Distant Signals," a man who is struggling with unemployment and the COVID pandemic moves into the home of his late parents. He reminisces about the unsettling and confusing children's television show that he watched as child, "Distant Signals," which he has never been able to learn anything about—until he finds videotaped recordings of it scattered through the house. Glen Hirshberg's "Destinationland" features another childhood obsession, in this case a small amusement park that features vintage decommissioned trains and one operating train ride. The narrator tells the story of the day he learned the secret of Destinationland, and the more horrifying secret that lay behind it.

Sasha Geffen's "Pastiche" is a tale of high school love, loss, and horror, featuring a student who occupies three bodies at once, in a manner that is tolerated by his classmates and teachers as well as can be done—until one day a line is irrevocably crossed. In Steve Rasnic Tem's "Privacy," a man has cut himself off from the outside world, ignoring his phone, computer, and television as much as possible—until one day refugees arrive on his house doorstep during what may very well be the end of the world.

As revealed in the editor's afterword, *Mooncalves* is a labor of love whose concept was born in the bleak events of 2020. The madness of the present and the uncertainty of the future pushed Thompson to create an anthology that reflected the times we lived in, and he sought out stories that captured that unsettling sense of the unknowable. Inspired by Ellen Datlow's *Best of the Year* anthologies, and in consultation with Adam Golaski, Thompson assembled *Mooncalves* from known authors he felt are underappreciated and others who are overlooked. The result is a self-funded compilation of stories that are unsettling, mystifying, and baffling—and I again mean that as the highest compliment. *Mooncalves* serves not only as an excellent anthology but as a snapshot of emotions that its authors felt over the past few turbulent years.

The Cabinet of Dr. del Toro

Michael D. Miller

Guillermo del Toro's Cabinet of Curiosities. 2022. Netflix.

Anticipation and excitement were running high after Netflix announced the release of the anthology horror series *Guillermo del Toro's Cabinet of Curiosities*. Those reactions were duly met, as it had been some time since a series of this sort graced itself on our televisions, *Masters of Horror* being the last one of note that I recall. And with genre veteran Guillermo del Toro at the helm, what could go wrong? The success of a series like this is highly important to the weird fiction field where, like short story anthologies, the genre thrives on that sustained unity-of-effect Poe articulated as only satisfied in a short sitting. We can all agree that we need a return of a strong regular horror-generating series such as *The Twilight Zone, The Outer Limits,* and *Tales from the Darkside*.

The series uses a very effective hook, or engine, a cabinet of curiosities, to spawn episode after episode. In this ornate antique display case holding mysterious shelves and strange miniature curios with obscure trinkets, del Toro prefaces each episode, randomly showing us an object that corresponds to the theme of each story, introduces the writer and director, then the camera takes us through the twisted menagerie of the cabinet credit sequence and into the opening scene. These "cabinets of wonder" or "wonder-rooms" dating back to the sixteenth century were initially rooms dedicated to various subjects, natural history, geology, archaeology, religion . . . they contained artifacts or relics of the various owners from their travels abroad. At the height of such popularity, they were symbols of status (no matter how outlandish or fake the objects often were), and today there is a revival of these in tiny museums across the miles. One only need consider the popping up of "obscura museums" boasting real artifacts from occultists and serial killers, the Oddities and Curiosities Expo touring across the county, and the popularity of Dr. Mütter's

Marvels Museum in Philadelphia.

The first tale of eight is "Lot 36" directed by del Toro's director of photography Guillermo Navarro and written by del Toro and the first of many TV series hacks, Regina Corrado (*The Strain*). The episode delivers an engaging scenario, that of the storage lot auction of contents from deceased renter's units to the highest bidder. The highest bidder in this case is a deplorable opportunist named Nick Appleton (Tim Blake Nelson), who makes his living pillaging these posthumous vaults and then cutting the seller in on the deal so that he automatically wins the bid. The deceased owner of Lot 36 was a Satanist who imprisoned a demon in the vault; it would be released if certain precautions are not taken when rummaging through the contents.

This story takes this usual religious horror trope and mixes it with cosmic/divine justice that we usually behold in most E.C. Comics and classic horror—a morally corrupt protagonist receives their just reward. In the case of Nick Appleton, he happens to be an unrepentant anti-immigrant racist willing to ignore the misfortunes of others so long as he makes his living. The story is set in the 1980s amid the immigration panic (contrasted with today's border crisis). Amelia (Elpidia Carrillo), the Mexican-American daughter of an earlier deceased owner whose lot Appleton has pillaged, learns the lot was auctioned by mistake and simply wants the family photos. Appleton tells her to go back to her country. In due course, when Appleton's exploits trigger the demon one night while rummaging through Lot 36, he is chased to a dead end where Amelia (who has remained outside the storage building) could let him out through a bolted door, but decides to ignore Appleton's pleas; the demon takes its sacrifice and Amelia laughs. The problem here is that, whereas Amelia could rise above Appleton's behavior, she deals it back to him, thus being no moral superior. The divine retribution is really disguised payback and sells the story and its political messaging short. Since Appleton is a truly unsympathetic character, this does not amount to any real sense of justice.

Taking the "divine justice" trope more seriously is episode number two, "Graveyard Rats"—based on the classic Henry

Kuttner story. Del Toro pens the script again, with the director of *The Cube,* Vincenzo Natali. David Hewlett plays Masson, the corrupt caretaker who pillages corpses for profit, including using some of that to pay off his debts to the mob. Complicating his little racket is a rat problem, a big one. An apparent infestation of giant rats is growing under his cemetery, and they are stealing bodies—and their personal effects. Masson's very livelihood is in peril. The difference between Masson and Nick Appleton is that we sympathize for Masson just enough to care. He is at the end of his rope; if he doesn't pay up to the crime thugs, he's dead. There's no one to help, local rat catchers included. What follows is Masson's trek into the rat tunnels, a veritable dungeon crawl through the horror of claustrophobia, where Masson encounters evidence of his past crimes, undead corpses, and of course one giant and convincing mutated rat god. Through it all, Masson tries to escape (while pocketing the occasional coin). We can relate to that. But as cosmic retribution takes its course, we know there is no escape for Masson, or us, and the doom ending resonates effectively.

Going beyond "Graveyard Rats" is episode number three, "The Autopsy," adapted from the clever Michael Shea story. The overarching theme so far, the stronger the source material, the more successful the episode, and this episode is the standout of this cabinet in that regard. Del Toro and David S. Goyer (*Blade II*) team up to adapt the tale. David Prior (*The Empty Man*) directs. Without spoiling this detective-story-meets-cosmic-noir plot, "The Autopsy" is full of wit, irony, dramatic reversals, and intrigue, leaving us on the edge of our seats the entire sequence. The story is the only episode of this series that reverses the doomed-protagonist horror trope, a win for the earthgazers against the cold indifference of an alien antagonist. The "cosmic justice" here is the human race having the last laugh, which really is "justice" if we look at horror on the cosmic scale.

The plot of the story involves a well-known pathologist, Dr. Carl Winters, who is invited to perform an autopsy on a body found in mysterious circumstances at the behest of Sheriff Nate Craven, who sums this up as: "Carl, this is one of those nightmare specials. The kind you never get to the bottom of." Carl (played flawlessly by F. Murray Abraham) is the "Sherlock Holmes" of pathologists and not easily fooled. The alien possessing the corpse on the autopsy table learns that the hard way when attempting to possess Dr. Winters, resulting in one of the most riveting intellectual verbal combats in recent times, destined to be an iconic scene. The climax alone makes *Cabinet of Curiosities* a must-see. "The Autopsy" holds its thematic premise every minute, as best articulated by Dr. Winters in his defense, "What's the alternative? Can't do anything about it. We're all on the same conveyer belt, Nate. Some of us fall off a bit sooner than the rest, but . . . we're all heading for the same destination."

However, sad to report, the series goes on a bit of a downward spiral from here. Episode four, "The Outside," directed by Ana Lily Amirpour (*A Girl Walks Home Alone at Night*) and written by another miniseries hack, Haley Z. Boston (*Brand New Cherry Flavor*), non-hit producer Emily Carroll, and del Toro. Kate Micucci plays Stacey and Martin Starr plays her husband Keith. One of the best aspects of this episode is the marriage interplay between the couple, as it is clear Stacey is socially awkward, isolated, with a major psoriasis problem, and Keith treats Stacey as such, knowing what's best for her. They same situation transpires at the bank where Stacey is employed. Her all-female co-workers are part of a clique of successful, extroverted rebels tired of "mansplaining," and Stacey wants to be like them. Here is a thematic iteration of the horror story where protagonists are going to get what they want, wiping out everyone in their way and we laugh at the sick joke.

Early on we find Stacey's only social outlet is binge-watching TV, and soon enough she is captivated by an ad for a miracle cream, destined to imbue beauty and confidence. It isn't long before splurging plunges into buckets of this cream that Stacey is able to do away with her know-it-all husband and make herself the envy of the girls at work. It is a triumph of evil and insanity that should shock the viewer or jolt a laugh at the dark humor. However, this fails largely because we don't really understand how the weird/horror element works. What is this cream? What about the company that sold it to her? (The cream commercial actors break the fourth wall at one point, speaking directly to Stacey in the discomfort of her own living room.) We don't really know the answer and we should for the weird element to have a true effect. In the end, stylistically, it is at best Terry Gilliam-tinged zombie art far short of Aronofsky's *Requiem for a Dream,* which apparently influenced the narrative.

And now we get to what is largely the selling point of the series but in all honesty is an example of H. P. Lovecraft adaptations gone astray. "Pickman's Model," written by del Toro and another TV hack, Lee Patterson (*Colony*), do destruction to Lovecraft's story. Adding Keith Thomas (wow, a *Firestarter* remake!) brings nothing to the directing. Too many people do not understand horror or H. P. Lovecraft with sincerity. This version of "Pickman's Model" does not invoke fear in the least. The filmmakers seemed to have failed to understand that this story is about the setting, the city of Boston, and one of the great executions of urban horror based on existing reality. None of that atmosphere or mood is brought into the adaptation, thus there is no way to produce the slow buildup when we discover the truth of Pickman's model. One satisfying aspect is the casting of Crispin Glover as a thoroughly convincing Richard Upton Pickman. As the original story is not considered one of Lovecraft's best, and written in the second person, the adaptation errs by shifting the focus from the urban horror into developing the character and family of the narrator, thus robbing the episode of any weirdness it may have had. We can hope that Lovecraft sculptor Bryan Moore is more successful with his forthcoming adaptation of the tale.

"Dreams in the Witch House," written by Mike Watkins—another TV series hack (*Origin*)—and del Toro butcher Lovecraft's classic story, and not even Catherine Hardwicke (*Twilight*) and casting Rupert Grint (best known for playing "Ron Weasley" in the Harry Potter film franchise) as Walter Gilman can avert disaster. The approach to this episode is to use the transformation school of adaptation, where the filmmakers take a few key elements of a work and then make up (transform) the rest as they see fit. In this adaptation they eschew everything except the witch Keziah Mason and her rat familiar Brown Jenkin to the point where one might ask, why don't you just write your own story and title it something else? Well, because no one would care, but if you retain Lovecraft's name you can fool people to invest their time.

This is nothing new. Roger Corman did it by using Edgar Allan Poe's name on films that are clearly not based on his stories. Transformation is okay when the adaptation retains the theme of the original work. Lovecraft's story, again not one of his best, is about the transition of Gothic horror, in particular Hawthornean New England horror rooted in the Salem witch trails, to modern science/cosmic horror. The filmmakers have cut that out, giving us a Gothic tale of a fraught protagonist seeking occult powers to bring back a lost love. Does that sound Lovecraftian? Even the conversion of Brown Jenkin into an antagonist beyond the villainy even Lovecraft imagined does not breathe much life into this dead adaptation. Stuart Gordon's version (*Masters of Horror*) remains the finer example.

But in the cosmos there is balm as well as bitterness, and that balm is . . . episode number seven, "The Viewing," written and directed by Panos Cosmatos (*Mandy*). *Mandy* co-writer Aaron Stewart-Ahn receives credit, as does del Toro. In fact, del Toro receives writing credit on all episodes, making us wonder if that isn't just part of the deal. Anyway, "The Viewing" is a return to greatness, a visual tour de force of atmosphere, mood, and annihilation so potent you'll only dare to view it once. Despite the fact that most of the episodes have "the Netflix look," the cinematography that seems to use the same color palette and looks as if they were shot by the same director, Cosmatos puts an end to such lack of vision. "The Viewing" has a style and tone all its own. In a simple plot, we are loaded into the chamber of the narrative and shot point-blank into an unforgettable hallucinatory acid trip. In short, reclusive billionaire Lionel Lassiter (played very cool by Peter Weller) invites a select group of socialites to his secluded mansion for "a viewing." After introducing themselves and partaking in a plethora of powerful drugs, Lassiter remarks, "Everyone has two lives, the second life begins the moment you realize that all along you only had one." Lassiter then takes them all into a room to view a meteorite about to hatch. And without wasting a film splice, the demon alien rock opens, unleashing havoc on the guests, including Lassiter, who isn't spared a gore-splattered end. To quote one of the characters, "Did this just happen?" Yes, it did. A true evocation of mood, atmosphere, and cosmic destruction delivered with little character and plot, the way it should be, with a slight David Cronenberg touch that comments directly on the act of viewing cinema itself.

Sadly, episode eight ends the series with a pitiful low. "The Murmuring" (and does it murmur) is written by del Toro and Jennifer Kent. Kent also directs, and with all the promise she has from her debut *The Babadook,* her skill cannot save this dud. There is no need to dwell much on what transpires. A couple suffering the recent loss of a child take a vacation to grieve and recover their relationship. They happen to be ornithologists, although I am not sure what that means symbolically except something to do with bird (specifically starling) murmuration. It follows the standard trope of placing a despairing couple into a haunted house that will test their love. This trope typically unfolds with the supernatural element bringing families closer or tearing them apart. The episode is an exercise in later Stephen King-style horror where the emphasis is on the human characters at the expense of the weird element, and that is why it fails. The same story could be told without a supernatural element, perhaps more convincingly. What "The Murmuring" does achieve is that it proves that this genre only works well when the focus is on the weird above everything else.

All in all, *Cabinet of Curiosities* is a must-see. What del Toro has given us is like a short story collection: every story isn't perfect, some rise to great heights and others fall short, but we have been given them. One can never fault the value of the filmed anthology series for the weird tradition. My hope is that future seasons look to more seasoned short story writers who know the form. There are plenty: Curtis M. Lawson, Gemma Files, Richard Gavin, Nicole Cushing, and Caitlín R. Kiernan to name a few. And for the love of cinema employ more visionary directors like Panos Cosmatos to weird us out beyond the point of no return.

Something of a Living Order

David Peak

THOMAS LIGOTTI. *Pictures of Apocalypse.* Illustrated by Jonathan Dennison. N.p.: Chiroptera Press, 2023. 110 pp. $70.00 hc. No ISBN.

Readers of this journal probably need no introduction to Thomas Ligotti. The man is nothing less than a legend, someone who has earned a spot in the pantheon of American horror alongside such luminaries as Robert W. Chambers, Edgar Allan Poe, H. P. Lovecraft, and Shirley Jackson. Considering Ligotti's towering stature, new material bearing his name is always cause for celebration.

That said, such material is increasingly infrequent. In fact, other than *Paradoxes from Hell,* a small collection of rare and unearthed poems and stories published by Chiroptera Press last year, Ligotti hasn't published a standalone edition of new material since *The Spectral Link* (Subterranean Press) in 2014. Today, most of us are resigned to knowing that not much unread material is forthcoming—something Ligotti himself seems to acknowledge in the first line of his introduction to this cycle of poems: "For good or ill, all things must end."

Ligotti goes on to describe the inevitable disappointment of a given picture of apocalypse, how such an event likely won't—or simply can't—live up to our expectations. Of course the famously pessimistic Ligotti would find some way to be disappointed by the end of humanity, lamenting in his inimitable, dry tone how it won't be big enough or fast enough or as spectacular as we have imagined.

In an interview in the *New Yorker* in 2015, he stated, "I tend to stipulate in my work that the world by its nature already exists in a state of doom rather than being in a process of doom."* With this in mind, the poems included in this col-

---

*www.newyorker.com/books/page-turner/the-horror-of-the-unreal

lection can be considered individual states of doom, one followed any another. They are poems that both wallow in fantasy and interrogate the function of that fantasy, poems that only Ligotti could write: equal parts morose, lyrical, and humorous.

"Great or small," Ligotti writes, referring to such apocalypses, "indefinite or definitive. They have already been inserted into existence, as built-in as breath and the end of breath."

* * *

The first thing you notice when you hold *Pictures of Apocalypse* is that it is a beautiful and lovingly designed book. The cover art and illustrations by Jonathan Dennison are extraordinary and lend the book a thoughtful cohesion. I can't overstate how good it feels just to hold this book, the satisfying weight of the paper stock, the saturation of the black ink. Honestly, the entire package more than justifies the book's perhaps shocking $70 price tag.

Similarly, the "pictures" that comprise this book betray a sense of cohesion, beginning with the aforementioned "end of an era" and finishing with a covenant—an agreement—made by a lone person standing watch over the end of the world.

Ligotti's poetic style tends to be straightforward. He often structures his poems as compact narratives, building out from a central conceit. The language is generally subdued, and the various forms tend to be rigid. Such constraints result in varying levels of success. Some poems tread familiar territory for Ligotti: "The Awakening," "I Anguish to the End," and "Turn and Turn About, Little Dolls." Others, particularly the shorter pieces such as "A Poetics of Existence," "Omega," and "Mystery" can feel undercooked.

That said, the longer, more imaginative pieces are often extraordinary—and for a variety of reasons. Consider, for instance, the menacing imagery and playful language of "The Cult of Melancholy":

> The sky above us was streaked with veins,
> winding like rivers of color, sickly pale,
> of snakes slowly writhing in the grayness—
> dying in sluggish spasms, spastic slithering,

iridescent rainbows left by corrosive tempests,
melting and ravaging annihilated landscapes.

And the austerity and control of "To No End":

It was a shame, we said,
it must end this way
in a place without time,
an end without end.

And the weary tone and economy of language of "Damn the Cost."

There is a toll we must pay
to a dark, malignant spirit,
a presence sensed but not seen
that appears at our birth
and follows us all our days.

The most successful poems, however, occur near the end of the book. Specifically, two poems, "Mental Notes on the End of Days" and "Two Visitations," extend Ligotti's famously dark vision and add new depth to his bleak world view. The former is an extended meditation on "the pageantry of portraiture," where the webwork of fractures in the paint give way to a hidden scripture, "a dark world that wildly flourishes."

And strange as it may seem, therein is a dimension of
   entities—
a universe that exists in tandem with our own, or what
   we call our own.
These practically invisible entities I would describe as
   specters with dead
eyes, although they are certainly not dead in the sense we
   use this term.
I know this, because when I look into those eyes they
   look back at me.

In this poem, Ligotti's language and imagery combine into the full force for which he is famous. It is a remarkably creepy piece, filled with occult obsession, paranoia, and dark wonder, which can be interpreted as perverting Nietzsche's warning of the monstrous "self" lacking a sense of art.

"Two Visitations," as the title suggests, is split into two parts. The first part, "The Bag," describes the anticipation of waiting in line to see a bag filled with "moving shadows that seem alive / not to mention sinister in some way." The second part, "The Tent," focuses on a carnival tent made with "something of a living order."

> You tremble with a sense of meaning,
> a feeling you have never known before,
> as the construction, the prodigy,
> spreads itself out and elevates,
> rising to the skies, higher and higher,
> throwing a shadow, an enveloping darkness,
> upon the treeless landscape and beyond.

The two pieces together are rich with detail and shimmering strangeness, both hinting at the mysteries of fascination and the horror of the cathedral of the world, that larger, perhaps invisible structure to which we are beholden.

* * *

Looking back over the centuries, hasn't it always been the case that lofty artistic heights are inspired by visions of apocalypse? What better subject matter could there be for a master author in the twilight of his career?

Overall, *Pictures of Apocalypse* is significantly more accomplished than Ligotti's 2004 poetry collection *Death Poems* (Bad Moon Books). Where that collection had a tendency to rely on cuteness rendered in flat language, this book offers more developed pieces rendered in rich prose. And where *Death Poems* was often limited by formal constraints, this book feels exploratory and free. There is no way around it: *Pictures of Apocalypse* is alive with wonder, wisdom, regret, and a bittersweet melancholy. Call these pieces *Life Poems,* if you will.

In this way, *Pictures of Apocalypse* truly feels like a successor to Ligotti's masterpiece long-form poems *I Have a Special Plan for This World* and *This Degenerate Little Town*. It builds upon the messages and themes of those poems—the beginning and the ending of this world and its many terrible shapes, all the worlds that have seeped from that ever-flowing source of death and decay—and carries these ideas through to their natural terminus.

If those earlier poems were about the destruction of worlds and the origin of rottenness, then *Pictures of Apocalypse* is about the fantasy of painless, grandiose annihilation. For that would be far too easy. And perhaps, Ligotti says, smirking in the shadows, that's what explains all those twilight masterpieces, all those biblical storms and hellscapes and congregations of angels. And then there's us, caught up in some twisted cosmic web, mere dolls, bemused and oh so entertained.

John William Polidori's *The Vampyre*

S. T. Joshi

[The following essay is scheduled to appear as liner notes to a spoken-word LP of Polidori's *The Vampyre,* to be issued by Cadabra Records.—Ed.]

The greatest literary contest in European history took place in the summer of 1816, when a group of writers gathered in a villa near Lake Geneva. If the result of the contest had been nothing but the writing of Mary Shelley's *Frankenstein,* it would have been notable enough; but another text—"The Vampyre," a long short story by John William Polidori—was also generated, and that work and its author prove to be of singular interest.

The short and generally unhappy life of Polidori is emblematic of an era that saw literary, artistic, and political figures blaze across the cultural sky like meteors, only to be snuffed out at the height of their powers. His family was of Italian origin; his father, Gaetano, had studied law and exhibited a literary bent. He came to England in 1791, seeking to escape the turmoil of revolutionary France, and married an Englishwoman, Anna Maria Pierce; they had eight children, the oldest of whom was John, born on September 7, 1795.

John was raised as a Catholic—a serious problem in an England that still inflicted civil penalties upon members of the faith. He was educated at a Benedictine monastery in York, but the curriculum was largely secular. At the age of thirteen he was already thinking of becoming a physician—either that, or a priest! He attended the University of Edinburgh, a notable institution for the study of medicine, from 1811 to 1815. His doctoral thesis was on the subject of somnambulism, which he associated with nightmares.

Polidori's multi-ethic background was the source of much social and cultural angst, as he could not decide whether his loyalties lay with the Italy of his ancestors or the England of his birth. In 1813 he flatly stated, "My disposition is not that of the English." Nonetheless, he began striking up an acquaintance with leading English writers of the period, including the poet Robert Southey and the social theorist Harriet Martineau.

George Gordon, Lord Byron (1788–1824) had heard of Polidori's medical skills through the literary grapevine. Feeling the need to have a physician in his company as he prepared for a trip to Europe (or "the Continent," as it was termed by the English), he decided to take Polidori along with him. It appears that Sir William Knighton, a physician, recommended Polidori to Byron. The poet's medical woes were largely the result of excessive drinking and the taking of opium (sometimes in the form of laudanum). By this time, Byron had already become the leading English poet of his time, even though such towering works as *Childe Harold's Pilgrimage* (1818) and *Don Juan* (1819–24) still lay in the future. Moreover, Byron was a flamboyant figure whose various antics (including a sexual affair with his half-sister Augusta) were the subject of appalled fascination throughout Europe. If Mick Jagger was a poet, he'd occupy the place in today's culture that Byron held in the Europe of the early nineteenth century.

Byron and Polidori, along with several others, set out on April 22, 1816, proceeding through the Netherlands and Germany to Lake Geneva. Polidori, in fact, does not seem to have been of much medical help to Byron. In Geneva they met up with Percy Bysshe Shelley and his entourage. This included the poet, his mistress Mary Wollstonecraft Godwin (Shelley was at this time still married; he would not marry Mary until the last day of 1816), and Claire Clairmont, a sometime mistress of Byron. They had left England on May 3.

Byron had rented the Villa Diodati, a mansion in the village of Cologny near Lake Geneva. It was apparently in June that Byron suggested a contest as to who could write the most chilling ghost story. The group had all been reading a work called *Fantasmagoriana; ou, Receuil d'histoires d'apparitions et spectres, revenans, fantômes, etc.* (1812; Fantasmagoriana; or, a Collection of Stories of Apparitions of Ghosts, Revenants, Phantoms, etc.), a French translation of some German ghost stories. The choice of subject matter for the contest is not at all surprising: the "Gothic novel" had burst upon the literary scene in the later eighteenth century. The movement was instigated by Horace Walpole, who wrote *The Castle of Otranto* (1764) and self-published it on his own printing press. Later, Ann Radcliffe (*The Mysteries of Udolpho,* 1794), Matthew Gregory Lewis (*The Monk,* 1796), Charles Robert Maturin (*Melmoth the Wanderer,* 1820) and many others contributed to the popularity of the form. In all, more than 400 Gothic novels were written between 1764 and 1820. The great majority of them have fallen into merited oblivion, and even the greatest of them cannot be said to be towering works of literature; but this was the first time that horror fiction became a bestselling genre.

Polidori mentions the contest in a diary entry of June 15, 1816. It appears that all four contestants began writing stories immediately. Nothing of Percy Shelley's, however, survives. This in itself is a little surprising: when he was a teenager he had written two short Gothic novels, *Zastrozzi* (1810) and *St. Irvyne* (1810), whose wretchedness is a prime instance of the adage that poets should stick to poetry. Mary, of course, eventually wrote *Frankenstein*. Byron wrote a fragment—alternatively titled "Fragment of a Novel" or "The Burial: A Fragment"—that bears some relevance to Polidori's "The Vampyre," as we shall see. Polidori's story was the first to be completed, although *Frankenstein* beat it into print, appearing in 1818 and being lauded by reviewers (including Sir Walter Scott) as a landmark. Given the prejudice against women prevailing at the time and for many years afterward, it was commonly assumed that Percy had assisted Mary significantly on the work, or perhaps wrote the work entirely and allowed his wife to receive credit for it; but there is now no reason to think that the work is anything but the work of Mary Shelley.

The Shelleys left the area at the end of August. Byron dismissed Polidori soon thereafter: his health had improved, and he saw no reason to keep the young physician at his side; in any case, they had quarreled frequently, and Byron was finding Polidori more and more of a nuisance. Polidori left on September 16 and went to Italy: he *walked* from Geneva to Milan, an arduous journey that took several weeks. Not surprisingly, he complained of having sore feet! But at last he had reached the land of his ancestors. He subsequently canvassed Milan, Florence, Pisa, Rome, Venice, and other locales in Italy. It was apparently at this time that he wrote or completed "The Vampyre." In various letters he said he wrote it in two or three days, "at the request of a lady." It was this lady (whoever she was) who instigated the next phase of the whole bizarre story.

The woman passed on the text to Henry Colburn, publisher of the *New Monthly Magazine*. There the story appeared as "The Vampyre: A Tale by Lord Byron" (!) in the April 1819 issue. Around the same time, the tale was published as a separate booklet, but with no author given. Polidori, to put it mildly, was annoyed. In writing to the publisher, he stated: "I . . . am sorry to find that your Genevan correspondence has led you into a mistake with regard to the tale of the Vampyre which is *not* Lord Byron's but was written *entirely* by me. . . . With regard to my own tale it is imperfect & unfinished I had rather therefore it should not appear in the magazine—and if the Editor had sent his communication as he mentions he would have been spared this mistake." A retraction was published in the next month's issue, with an accompanying letter by Polidori (although it appears that the wording of this letter was dictated by Colburn), in which he states that "your correspondent has been mistaken in attributing that tale, *in its present form,* to Lord Byron. The fact is, that though *the groundwork* is certainly Lord Byron's, its developement [*sic*] is mine."

There is much to untangle here. "The Vampyre" does indeed owe something of a debt to Byron's fragment, which similarly records a voyage undertaken by the narrator in the company of one Augustus Darvell. They go to Europe, then to the "East" (specifically Smyrna, a city in western Turkey that had been founded by the Greeks, and is mentioned in "The Vampyre"). At Ephesus, another Greek-founded city in Turkey, Augustus falls ill and dies; his face immediately turns black, suggesting some sort of poison. The fragment ends soon thereafter.

There is no suggestion at all that Augustus is a vampire.

The only critical element that Polidori took from the fragment was the vow that Augustus exacted from the narrator not to speak for a certain time of the events in which they had been involved. This element does indeed play a significant role in "The Vampyre," but the rest of the story is apparently the product of Polidori's imagination. Indeed, in disavowing his authorship of the story, Byron frequently stated that he had little knowledge of or interest in vampires.

It may not be entirely accurate to say that "The Vampyre" is the first significant treatment of the vampire myth in literature. The motif is, of course, of great antiquity, even though the English word "vampire" only dates to 1734. What is more, the vampire motif was enjoying considerable popularity in English and European poetry at the time. The first known poem specifically on the subject was Henrich August Ossenfelder's "Der Vampir" (1748). Samuel Taylor Coleridge's *Christabel* (written in 1797–1800) and John Keats's *Lamia* (1820) feature female vampire-like figures. Byron himself had treated the legend in passing in *The Giaour* (1813).

The story is based on the premise of two young men taking a "tour" of Europe—exactly as Byron and Polidori had done. Such a voyage was a common occurrence: the English, for all their patriotism, recognized a cultural inferiority to the great nations of Europe, especially those that had benefited from Greco-Roman culture, and they felt the need to augment their education by immersing themselves in the monuments of France, Italy, and Greece. Lord Ruthven, however, is depicted as a ruthless aristocrat—he gambles, corrupts youth, engages in robbery (of the wealthy), and so on. At one point his young, naïve companion, Aubrey (this is his surname; his first name is never given), prevents Ruthven from the "ruin of an innocent" (that is, Ruthven's deflowering a young unmarried woman).

It is in Greece that Aubrey meets Ianthe, a woman of "innocence, youth, and beauty," who tells him of "the living vampyre" who extends his life "by feeding upon the life of a lovely female." Her description of the vampire sounds a great deal like Lord Ruthven! Aubrey later finds himself at night in a wood thought to be a haven of vampires. He has an encounter with someone "whose strength seemed superhuman." He manages to repel the creature, but later finds that Ianthe is dead, having been drained of blood. Ruthven now reappears and helps Aubrey recover from his trauma. They presently resume their trip. They are beset by robbers; Ruthven is shot and wounded. He apparently dies; the robbers place him on the summit of a mountain, to be "exposed to the first cold ray of the moon." The body later disappears. Aubrey finds evidence that the person who attacked him and Ianthe was Lord Ruthven.

Aubrey returns to England. At a soirée where his sister is being "presented" (that is, formally introduced to society upon her coming of age), Ruthven seems to show up, seize his arm, and speak to him—then he vanishes. Aubrey sees Ruthven a few days later; clearly he wishes to take possession of Miss Aubrey. Months later Aubrey hears that his sister is engaged to the Earl of Marsden—but this is none other than Ruthven. Only after the marriage ceremony has taken place is Aubrey able to say that Ruthven is a vampire—but by then it is too late.

The tale has been frequently taken to be a not so subtle account of Polidori's own dealings with Lord Byron. The hints of a homosexual encounter in the story are matched by at least one passage in Polidori's diary where he may have had sex with the polymorphous nobleman. More significantly, the story begins laying out the "rules" for the manner in which a vampire functions. Blood-sucking to prolong one's life is the central motif; but many others that we now associate with the vampire—the inability to walk about in daylight; the need to preserve the soil of one's homeland as a place of repose during the day, and so on—were only introduced in later vampire literature, most notably in Bram Stoker's *Dracula* (1897). The fact that a vampire can be revived by moonlight was an element that eventually dropped out of the literary tradition, even though it is one of the few striking moments in James Malcolm Rymer's interminable *Varney the Vampire; or, The Feast of Blood* (1845–47).

Polidori's "The Vampyre" proved highly popular. The booklet was reprinted five times in 1819 alone. Its critical reception was mixed, although the great German poet Johann Wolfgang von Goethe incredibly believed that it was Lord Byron's masterpiece. In 1828 Heinrich Augustus Marschner composed an opera, *Der Vampyr,* with Sir Aubrey and Lord Ruthven as characters; but the work overall owes little to Polidori aside from these names.

The rest of Polidori's life can be told briefly. He suffered a serious head injury when his carriage overturned in September 1817. Although he managed to publish two books of poetry and a novel, *Ernestus Berchtold* (1819), he could never focus on a career, either as a writer or as a physician. In August 1821 he went to Brighton, gambled recklessly, then killed himself by poison on August 24.

But his association with Byron and the contest of 1816 gives him a place in literary history, and even in popular culture—if Ken Russell's over-the-top film *Gothic* (1986), in which the contest is portrayed luridly, with Polidori played by Timothy Spall, is any guide. "The Vampyre" may not be a masterwork, but its slow, gradual build-up to a cataclysmic conclusion argues for a literary skill that could have been developed had Polidori chosen to continue his life. As it is, he laid the groundwork for the vampire to stalk through the realms of literature, film, and other media, and that is surely immortality enough for anyone.

About the Contributors

Ramsey Campbell is an English horror fiction writer, editor, and critic who has been writing for well over fifty years. He is frequently cited as one of the leading writers in the field. His website is www.ramseycampbell.com.

Bobby Derie is the author of *Sex and the Cthulhu Mythos* (2014) and *Weird Talers: Essays on Robert E. Howard and Others* (2019). His essays have been published in the *Lovecraft Annual, The Dark Man: The Journal of Robert E. Howard and Pulp Studies, The Unique Legacy of* Weird Tales: *The Evolution of Modern Fantasy and Horror* (2015), *The* Weird Tales *Story: Expanded and Enhanced* (2021), *Robert E. Howard Changed My Life* (2021) and *Hither Came Conan* (2023).

Tony Fonseca is the library director at Elms College, in Chicopee, Massachusetts. He has published (under the name Anthony J. Fonseca) several books and articles on horror and dark literature, horror film, academic librarianship, musical film, and hip hop/rap music, and he co-owns the independent studio Dapper Kitty Music, which specializes in indie and meditative music.

Greg Gbur is a professor of physics and optical science at UNCC Charlotte. For more than a decade he has written a blog called *Skulls in the Stars* (skullsinthestars.com) about physics, horror fiction, and curious intersections between them. He has written a number of introductions to classic reprinted horror novels for Valancourt Books.

Alex Houstoun is a co-editor of *Dead Reckonings*. He has published *Copyright Questions and the Stories of H. P. Lovecraft,* available by contacting him at deadreckoningsjournal@gmail.com.

S. T. Joshi is the author of *The Weird Tale* (1990), *I Am Providence: The Life and Times of H. P. Lovecraft* (2010), *Unutterable Horror: A History of Supernatural Fiction* (2012), and other critical and biographical studies. A two-volume history of atheism is forthcoming from Pitchstone Publishing.

Michael D. Miller is a former professor of genre studies, currently writing reviews, articles, and poetry for the weird fiction genre with work appearing in *Dead Reckonings, Lovecraft Annual, Spectral Realms, Penumbra,* Alien Buddha Press, Dumpster Fire Press, and *Marchxness.* He is the author of the *Realms of Fantasy PRG* for Mythopoeia Games Publications.

David Peak's most recent book is *The World Below* (Apocalypse Party). His fiction has appeared in *Looming Low, Volume II* (Dim Shores) and *Year's Best Weird Fiction Volume Five* (Undertow Publications).

Daniel Pietersen is the editor of *I Am Stone: The Gothic Weird Tales of R. Murray Gilchrist,* part of the British Library's Tales of the Weird series. He is also a regular guest lecturer for the Romancing the Gothic project.

Géza A. G. Reilly is a writer and critic with an interest in twentieth-century American genre literature. A Canadian expatriate, he now lives in the wilds of Florida with his wife, Andrea, and their cat, Mim.

A career-retrospective of **Darrell Schweitzer's** short fiction was published by PS Publishing in two volumes in 2020. A veritable flood of Schweitzeriana is soon to follow from various publishers in the next year or so, including a new Lovecraftian anthology, *Shadows out of Time* (PS), *The Best of* Weird Tales: *The 1920s* (Centipede Press), *The Best of* Weird Tales *1924* (with John Betancourt; Wildside Press), a weird poetry collection, *Dancing Before Azathoth,* a new story collection, *The Children of Chorazin* (Hippocampus Press), and two further volumes of author interviews (Wildside Press). He was co-editor of *Weird Tales* between 1988 and 2007.

Joe Shea (The joey Zone) is an artist and illustrator. Samples of his work can be found at www.joeyzoneillustration.com.

Oliver Sheppard is a poet based in Texas. He is the author of the Elgin Award nominated *Thirteen Nocturnes* and writes for *Post-Punk(dot)com, CVLT Nation,* and others.

Clark Tucker is a volunteer proofreader for Hippocampus Press. He lives in Western Massachusetts and can be reached at clarkhorror1@gmail.com.